LIVE ♥ LIFE
ABERDEENSHIRE

livelifeaberdeenshire.org.uk/libraries

Chapter 1

~Bertha~

10th April 1912

When the steam whistles blasted, Bertha jumped so hard she was almost catapulted off the deck. The whistles sounded again and she stuffed her fingers in her ears. Her mother rapped her on the arm with the umbrella she'd insisted on carrying, "*in case of spring showers*".

'Stop that, dear. You'll ruin your new gloves and it doesn't look at all ladylike.'

Bertha turned from the rail and gave her mother a wicked grin.

'It might be ladylike in America. And so might whistling... and climbing trees... and spitting in the street!'

Her mother snorted, in a rather unladylike fashion. 'I hardly think so.'

But her mother didn't know. Neither of them knew how American ladies behaved. Her mother was as much at sea as she was. They didn't know the rules. Perhaps there were none. Bertha hugged herself, enjoying the warmth and softness of her new fur-lined coat. She could hardly wait. Her life was about to change. In America, everything was going to be different.

Bertha leant over the rail, feeling giddy. The ground looked such a long way down.

All around them, people were waving caps or handkerchiefs, calling farewells. Down on the quay, a massive crowd waved back, jostling for space, craning their necks to spot their friends and relatives, or simply to goggle at the size of the ship.

But something else was going on. A group of men, kit bags on their shoulders, were pushing their way through the crowd, heading towards one of the gangways. They were yelling, waving their arms.

'Oi, hold on, we're coming aboard!'

Bertha bent double over the rail. She might have toppled, if Rosa Pinsky, who was sharing their cabin, hadn't grabbed her coat collar.

'They're stokers by the look of them,' said Mrs Pinsky dismissively, as if stokers were unimportant, an optional extra on a steam ship. 'And they've had one too many beers in the public house, I expect.'

The men had reached the edge of the dock. But the officer shook his head, held them back with a raised arm. The lower gangway was pulled back and the would-be crew members were left stranded on the shore, shaking their fists, cursing. Bertha filed away their most colourful swear words, thinking they might be useful in her exciting new life.

Behind her, Mrs Pinsky gasped, and for a second, Bertha worried that she'd accidentally sworn aloud. It was far too soon. The ship hadn't even left the dock yet. They were still in Britain, with its million rules and regulations about how well brought up girls should behave.

'Do you see that?" asked Mrs Pinsky, in her wonderfully exotic Polish/American accent. 'One of those stokers dodged the officers! He's on the steerage gangway, see?'

Bertha looked to where Rosa was pointing, and saw a stocky man with fiery red hair, shoving his way past the last of the 3rd Class passengers, moving with such determination that he almost pushed a young lad into the water. As he reached the ship, the red-haired man stopped, looked back, and then vanished inside.

'No wonder the rest are so annoyed,' said Bertha's mother. 'They have missed the boat, and no mistake!' She beamed, enjoying her own joke. 'It's a dreadful shame.' Bertha clutched at her heart, imitating a film actress she'd seen at the Star Picture Palace. 'Imagine how disappointed they must be. They thought they were about to start a fabulous new job on the finest ship in the world!'

'Shovelling coal into furnaces day and night isn't my idea of fabulous!' snorted Ellen Toomey. 'It'll be like the pits of Hell down there in the boiler rooms.'

Bertha opened her mouth, about to tell Ellen that actually, it was rude to interrupt, but closed it when she noticed her mother's warning frown. She had a sneaking suspicion Miss Toomey's interruptions might become a regular occurrence. The Irish woman, who was sharing their cabin too, didn't seem to have much time for her, and they'd only been acquainted a matter of hours. But Bertha had no intention of allowing Ellen to spoil a single moment.

She gave a heartfelt sigh.

'Those men were headed on a wonderful voyage across the Atlantic Ocean, and now the poor souls are going nowhere.'

The men's disappointment wasn't hard for her to imagine, because three days ago, her mother had informed her that the ship they'd planned to travel on, the *New York*, wasn't going to sail after all, because of a coal strike. Bertha had been totally devastated.

'We can't go back to Aberdeen!' she'd wailed. 'Please, you know we can't go back. We've sold the house. We've got to find a ship that will take us to America. Poor Daddy is all alone.'

This might have been true, but when Bertha had sobbed into her pillow that night, she hadn't wept for her father, who seemed from his letters to be perfectly happy and enjoying his work as an architect in Portland,

Oregon. Her tears had been for her own crushed dreams.

The run up to leaving home had been hard. When she'd hugged her school friends goodbye, she'd been painfully aware that she'd probably never see them again. But even as she'd wept, and promised to write— even when she'd handed over her precious collection of china dolls to her best friend Jean—excitement had been bubbling inside her, hot as magma.

Her life was about to change. This was her *Big Adventure.* She was leaving all the greyness... cloudy skies, the granite buildings, her boring, humdrum life behind. In America she could reinvent herself, or at least become a more confident, glamorous, grown-up version of herself. How could she bear to go back, to resume her childish routine of school and church and Sunday school?

She'd cried herself to sleep, distraught that the *Big Adventure* was over, when it had hardly begun.

But yesterday her life had been saved. She'd been in the parlour of her uncle's London townhouse, playing a game of marbles with her three cousins, while trying to eavesdrop on her mother's and aunt's conversation, when the door had been flung open and her uncle had barged in, beaming and waving two large pieces of paper.

'Oh Bessie, you're in luck. I've got passage on a new ship for you. And I mean a new ship. Brand spanking new. This trip to New York will be her maiden voyage.

Have you guessed the name of it?'

He'd handed her mother the ticket with a flourish, as if she were the Queen. Then he'd given Bertha hers, with rather less ceremony. She'd examined it, reading aloud, excitement and nerves bubbling in her stomach.

'I don't believe it! We're travelling on the finest steamer in the world!'

Her uncle had laughed, enjoying her reaction.

'So say the White Star Line. They are calling her the Queen of their fleet.'

He'd turned back to Bertha's mother.

'And the newspapers have declared her *"practically unsinkable"*. You'll be relieved to hear that, Bessie, I'm sure!'

Bertha had glanced at her mother, suddenly anxious; the possibility of the ship sinking hadn't even occurred to her. But her mother had smiled, as wide as the ocean. She'd flung her arms around her brother's neck.

'Thank you, thank you so much! James will be so relieved. Our wee family has been apart for six months and thanks to you, we will be together at last. Look, Bertha! The ship leaves tomorrow. Finally, we are off to New York!'

Bertha's fingers had trembled as they'd traced the black letters:

RMS Titanic

We're leaving. The Big Adventure is actually happening.

Dull, mousy me is getting left behind. Goodbye, boring wee Bertha. Howdy, Robertha Watt, pioneering adventuress.

As boarding finished and the crew began hauling up the lines, Bertha felt excitement building in her chest. The steam whistles sounded again, signalling to the group of tugboats which chugged around the massive ship. Slowly, majestically, the *Titanic* began to move away from Berth Number 44.

'We're off,' she breathed, tugging at her mother's sleeve. 'We're going to see Daddy at last! Do you think he'll recognise me?'

Her mother tutted. She was a sensible, level-headed woman, who didn't have time for "*dramatics*" and even less for "*hysteria*" She was determined that Bertha would indulge in neither but was often disappointed.

'Stop your nonsense, Bertha. Of course he will.'

Ellen Toomey must have overheard, because she stopped chatting to Mrs Pinsky, pointed at Bertha and laughed: a harsh bark, like a fox's. 'Your Daddy will recognise you by those teeth in an instant.'

Heat burned Bertha's cheeks. Her hand flew to her face, covering her mouth.

'Tosh! He will know you by that beautiful auburn hair.' Rosa Pinsky's sympathetic eyes only made Bertha feel worse. 'And by those lovely dark eyes.'

There was an almighty bang. Ellen Toomey screeched

7

like a barn owl and Bertha's first thought was that Ellen deserved her fright for being so mean. But then fear gripped her too, because she could see something terrible was happening. One of the docked ships seemed to have broken its moorings. It was drifting across the water, pulled towards the *Titanic*, like iron filings to a magnet.

'Gracious!' gasped her mother. 'The *New York* is coming straight for us!'

When even her mother sounded alarmed, Bertha knew they were in big trouble. Her heart banged against her ribs as she watched the stern of the American liner swing towards the *Titanic*. It seemed deeply strange that the ship they'd originally booked for their voyage, the ship that was going nowhere, was now drifting ever closer. One way or another, the *New York* seemed determined to stop her from travelling.

What if the newspapers are wrong? What if the ship sinks and we all have to swim to shore? What if my mother decides she's had enough adventure and takes me back to Aberdeen?

Tears stung her eyes and she wiped them away with her glove.

It wasn't that she'd disliked Ashley Road School. The teachers were strict but fair, and she'd excelled at gymnastics and creative writing. But she'd said all her goodbyes. She'd cut the cords that had bound her to school and home and Belmont Congregational Church. She was ready to fly... or at least to set sail, as her mother had laughed at Bertha's suggestion they go by airship.

Don't be silly, dear. Those dirigibles are far too dangerous for transatlantic crossings. We'll be much safer on an ocean liner.

Bertha wondered if those words were echoing in her mother's head at this very moment.

The *New York* was only feet from them; a collision seemed inevitable. When Bertha looked over the rail at the frothy grey waves heaving below her, nausea rose in her throat, and she breathed a silent prayer.

Please God, I want to get to America. I don't want to go home. Please don't let this be the end.

Chapter 2

Johan

10th April 1912

Johan hadn't bothered to stand for long at the Poop Deck's railings. Nobody he knew had come to see him off. His mother, sister Anna and younger brothers were all at home in Sweden. His father and older sister Jenny were in South Dakota, awaiting his arrival.

For the first time in his life, he was totally alone and although everyone around him seemed to be in a celebratory mood, his guts churned with homesickness and fear. When a rowdy group of girls had hurled themselves against the railings, yelling raucous farewells to their loved ones on the dock, he'd allowed himself to be jostled out of the way, and had wandered off. He'd found an iron ladder to lean against, and pulled his cap down low, so that nobody would notice he was crying.

The whistling, whooping and cheering had gone on and on, even after the ship had slipped away from its berth, but in the last few moments, the atmosphere had changed. Something terrible was happening, he could tell. There had been an ear-splitting bang, and all the jollification had stopped. People were tense, watching. Somebody was yelling in what might have been Italian. He couldn't be sure, because he didn't speak Italian. There were lots of fellow Swedes on this ship, he knew that, but not being able to understand the majority of the passengers was one of the many things making him homesick, longing to be back in his village, where everyone was familiar and spoke the same dialect.

But he needed to know what disaster had befallen the ship, so he wiped the tears from his cheeks, and walked back towards the railings.

It was hard to see past the jostling crowd and not for the first time Johan cursed his lack of height. It was typical bad luck; Swedish men were meant to have tall, athletic builds. Though at fourteen, he wasn't quite a man yet, his new jacket had plenty of growing room.

'Excuse me,' he said, in English. His father had said in his last letter that Johan must strive to become fluent in English, but he hadn't made it clear who should teach him. There weren't many polyglots about in Knared, and none prepared to tutor for free. He'd picked up "*excuse me*", "*sorry*", "*please*" and "*how much?*" on the boat to Hull, although he'd spent most of that horrible journey hanging over the side, puking into the choppy grey sea.

In the same letter, Pa had also suggested that when he reached South Dakota it might be best if Johan changed his name to John. He didn't say why, but it didn't make

Johan feel any happier about leaving Sweden for America, where even his name didn't seem to be acceptable.

He tried again to get past the crowd at the railing.

'Excuse me. Please.'

Nobody moved. Either this lot didn't speak English either or else they were choosing to ignore him.

Determined to see what was going on, Johan elbowed his way past a thin faced woman carrying a baby, her other three children clinging to her skirts, squawking like chickens. Then he pushed past an elderly couple, who seemed frozen in shock and didn't react at all when Johan reached the rail and leaned over it, right in front of them.

When he saw the problem, his grip on the railing tightened so much his fingers turned white. A ship was drifting towards the *Titanic*, getting ever nearer. He'd noticed the ship earlier, tied to another, larger vessel, like a pup chained up to its Ma. Now, the smaller beast had escaped its chains. The series of bangs must have been the hawsers giving way as the *Titanic* accelerated past.

The two boats were going to collide. Johan held his breath, waiting for the crunch, the scream of tearing metal. When the crash came, a gaping hole would be ripped in Titanic's hull. The tiny hairs on the back of his neck rose.

He squeezed his eyes shut, and prayed.

Please God, let the ships crash. Nobody will get hurt.

Most will be able to swim to shore. It's not far. We can put the old folks and the little ones on all those lifeboats hanging off the side of the ship. Please God, let the boats crash, so I can go home.

Johan opened his eyes, and decided God didn't speak Swedish either.

A squat little tugboat was chugging through the water. Its skipper threw a line up to the drifting liner. Smoke billowed from the tug's funnel as it strained against the weight of the much larger vessel. Johan watched, cursing the skipper under his breath. With any luck, he thought, the tug's efforts would be in vain.

He remembered when he was small, gripping the rope round the neck of their elkhound, Einar, struggling to prevent the determined beast from chasing sheep. He'd had to drop the rope in the end, as his hands were burnt and his arms were being pulled from their sockets. Einar had frightened the pregnant ewes, and he'd got the blame. He wondered who would get the blame for this mess. Not him, this time at least. He'd swim back to the dock, catch a boat back to Knared, write to his father, tell him he'd been unable to sail, through no fault of his own, and he'd come later, with the rest of the family, when they'd saved the money.

But luck wasn't with him. His heart sank as he saw another tug chugging towards the ships, on its way to help the first. Somehow the tiny boats held on to the liner, slowed its drift.

A man on the deck shouted in Swedish.

'*Allt ar bra!*'

All is well... and it was. Miraculously, with four feet to spare, the Titanic skimmed past the other ship. A collision had been avoided; disaster averted.

As the great liner glided out on to Southampton Water, and all around him people cheered, Johan let out a hiss of frustration.

This voyage wasn't over, after all.

Johan didn't hang around on the Poop Deck. He remembered the anger in the eyes of the red-haired man and was worried that he might come looking for him. Going by the fiddle music and the stomping feet, there seemed to be a party going on in the 3rd Class Common Room, so he didn't enter, but crept back to the cramped cabin and crouched on his mattress, gazing listlessly at the three empty bunks. It didn't feel safe, sharing a room with strangers—even if they were Swedish. Why did he have to cross the ocean on his own? It wasn't fair. Fear made his stomach cramp and he needed to use the toilet, but he wasn't sure where the facilities might be. Maybe he'd have to do his business over the side of the ship?

To take his mind off his worries, he focused instead on the positive: the treasure hidden in the lining of his jacket.

Sliding one hand inside his jacket, Johan ran his

fingers across the lining, feeling the tight stitches and the ridges of the coins. His mother was responsible for those coins: fifteen kroner, more money than he'd ever owned. He closed his eyes, so he could picture her, sitting by the stove, fingers darting as she sewed. He could hear the worry in her voice.

'They're for emergencies only. Don't use them aboard ship. You won't need them if you're frugal. Your food is included in the price of your ticket. The money's for when you get to New York... and only then if you're in real need. Otherwise, give them to your father when he collects you.'

Johan pulled a face. Over his cold, dead body was that going to happen! If Pa knew the money existed, and demanded it, he'd claim to have been robbed on board ship rather than hand it over. His father would want it for corn, or cattle feed, but this money had been earned by his mother, selling her crafts at the local market: colourful rag rugs, woollen mittens, and little Christmas angels woven from straw.

Before his father even had the chance to ask, he'd bury the coins under a tree in South Dakota and give them back to his mother when she arrived in America, so she could buy herself a new dress for her new life, or a big hat like all the ladies in 1st Class wore, though he imagined his sensible mother would prefer a comfortable, well made dress to one of those daft, impractical hats. How those silly women could see where they were going, with their view obscured by bunches of flowers and trailing ostrich feathers, he couldn't fathom.

The thought of the money reminded him that he might just have come into some more. Shoving a hand inside his trouser pocket, his fingers grasped a crumpled ball of paper.

He pulled it out.

Finders, keepers, he whispered.

When the train had arrived at the dockside at nine thirty that morning, Johan had been so shattered that he'd gone for a kip on a bench and had only jerked awake when a steam whistle had blasted. He'd leapt up, heart racing, convinced he was going to miss the boat and be in the trouble of his life, but when he'd run towards the 3rd Class gangway there were people still queuing.

As he'd waited on the gangway, he'd seen a group of broad shouldered crew men, trying in vain to be allowed to board. One of them, a short, stocky fellow with bright red hair, had veered to the left and scrambled up the 3rd Class gangway, towards the stragglers. As he shoved past Johan, nearly toppling him off the gangway, the paper ball had dropped from his jacket pocket and bounced towards the water.

Johan caught the ball mid-bounce and scooped it into the safety of his pocket. It must have caught the man's eye, because he'd turned around. Johan had held the paper ball up, ready to throw it back to him, but the man had looked straight at him, shaking his head. He must have realised he was too far away to catch it. The irate officer had been on his tail, so he'd kept running, through the entrance and onto the ship, ahead of Johan and the other passengers. The look he'd given Johan before he'd fled had rattled the boy. If looks could kill, he'd have been dead. It had annoyed him too—he was only trying to help. So he'd stuffed the ball of paper into his own pocket; it was his property now.

The humiliation of the medical examination had pushed the incident to the back of Johan's mind. As he'd stepped aboard ship, it had dawned on him why the queue had been moving so slowly; all of the 3rd Class passengers were being examined, their eyes checked for infection, their heads for nits, being treated like cattle at an auction. When the medical officer had yanked up his eyelid with a button hook, he'd pretended it didn't hurt at all. When he'd been ordered to stick out his tongue, he'd held his head high, and glared, but he'd felt shame burning his cheeks. The doctor had seemed unfazed by his anger, and just handed him an Inspection Card telling him to move along.

Now that Johan had a moment's privacy he could take a proper look, see what he'd salvaged. He carefully unfolded the paper, his heart sinking as he did. He'd been hoping it might be a bank note, but no such luck. It was just a torn fragment of writing paper.

I might have known. Nothing's going my way lately.

But as he pulled the ball apart, something fell out, landed on the straw mattress, and nestled there, glinting. He picked the object up; it was a tiny, silver key. He twirled it between his thumb and forefinger, excitement beating a drum in his chest. Glancing around, just in case he was being watched, he slipped the key into his top pocket of his jacket and took a closer look at the paper.

One side was a letter by the look of it, in loopy, untidy writing, in an unfamiliar language which Johan figured might be English, like every sign on this stupid ship. It infuriated him that little thought seemed to have been given to the fact there were hundreds of passengers on board who couldn't speak English, never mind read it.

But the other side was more interesting. Someone had drawn all over it, a rough sketch, intersecting lines, a flurry of arrows.

Johan turned the paper over in his hands, attempting to decipher it.

Perhaps it's a treasure map. Please let it be a treasure map.

If this was a treasure map—if he could find the treasure—he could buy tickets for his mother and his five brothers and sisters to come over to South Dakota too. First class tickets, so they could travel in style.

They'd be able to hire labourers to help on the farm. He'd get himself a horse and trap, or maybe a motor car. Everything would be alright, after all.

All he had to do was find somebody who'd help him read this map.

Chapter 3

Bertha

10th & 11th April 1912

Bertha spent her first afternoon aboard ship in a whirl of exploration, checking out the splendid facilities in 2nd Class: the Library, the Dining Saloon, and the impressive oak-panelled Smoking Room. She didn't enter the Smoking Room, only peered inside, as it appeared to be for men only. Bertha took this as evidence that American ladies didn't smoke, which was good news as far she was concerned. Her uncle smoked cigars and they stank to high heavens. It wasn't a habit in which she had any desire to indulge.

The facilities were very impressive, although sadly not in comparison to the 1st Class facilities, of which they'd been allowed a brief tour before the ship sailed.

Bertha had been enchanted by the Grand Staircase, with its massive glass and wrought iron dome and glittering crystal chandelier. She'd walked up a few steps, running one hand over the smooth polished oak banister, and then floated back down towards the bronze cherub sculpture with its illuminated torch, all the while imagining herself as a famous film star, in a silk gown, tiara and fur stole, waving graciously to her awestruck audience, until her mother had brought her back to earth with a thud.

'Stop it, Bertha. You're making a show of yourself.'

Bertha had stomped down the last few steps.

'When I'm grown up, I shall have a staircase like this one in my house,' she'd insisted. 'But mine will have a statue of a silver mermaid at the base.'

Rosa had winked, and nudged Bertha's elbow.

'Better set your cap at young Billy Carter in 1st Class then. The whole Carter family is on board and they're all as rich as Croesus.'

Heat had crept up Bertha's face. 'Marianne Dashwood, my absolute favourite Jane Austen character, said that "*setting one's cap at a man*" is a particularly odious cliché.'

Rosa Pinsky had laughed, but Bertha's mother had been affronted.

'Bertha Watt, mind your manners!' she'd snapped, but Bertha hadn't finished.

'Besides, I have no intention of marrying, for money or otherwise. I shall make my own fortune, by my own means, thank you very much, as a film actress, a polar explorer—or both.'

Then she'd closed her mouth before her mother lost the rag with her completely.

But even Bertha's mother had been impressed by the

Grand Staircase, and it took a lot to impress Bessie Watt.

'It certainly deserves its title,' she'd mused, as the tour ended. 'I suspect the 2nd Class staircases will seem rather pedestrian in comparison.'

Miss Toomey had snorted.

'They're showing us how the other half live. And then snatching it away.'

By the time the ship arrived at the harbour at Cherbourg, Bertha had finished as much of her self-guided tour as the stewards would permit, and was back to leaning over the railing, hopping from one foot to another in excitement at the prospect of landing in France. But when the engines stopped and the ship dropped anchor, they were still far from shore.

'Why have we stopped so far out?' she asked a passing steward. 'I was hoping to go ashore, just for a minute, so I could tell the folks back home that I'd visited France.'

The deckhand laughed, not unkindly.

'She's too big to go right into the harbour. See those small boats? They're called tenders, and they're going to take off the few passengers whose journeys are ending and bring the new passengers aboard. Nearly three hundred more, I believe, including a couple of American millionaires, who I'm hoping are good tippers.'

It was quite disappointing news, but when the ship set off again, Bertha stood on the Boat Deck, her long ringlets pulled into tangles by the wind, promising herself she'd visit France properly one day. After all, she was a seasoned traveller already. Train from Aberdeen to London, several hansom cabs whilst in the capital, early train to Southampton and now aboard the biggest ship in the world.

The following morning the ship reached Queenstown in Ireland, and again, to Bertha's disappointment, the ship anchored two miles out. She stood on the Boat Deck, enjoying the bright sunshine, watching as another hundred or so passengers, mainly 3rd Class, were brought aboard by tender. More excitingly, some other small boats sailed out to the Titanic too, loaded with lace and other crafts. They set up stalls, and for a couple of hours sold their wares aboard the ship, though Bertha had no money of her own and couldn't persuade her mother to buy a single thing. It wasn't a complete waste of time though, as she managed to persuade several passengers to sign her autograph book.

'Look at this signature!' She pushed the book under her mother's nose. 'John Jacob Astor IV! I asked him for it while he was buying a lace shawl for his wife. The seller must have charged him a fortune because he was handing over a lot of bank notes. His wife is only eighteen, you know, and Mr Astor looks ancient!'

'She married him for his money, I don't doubt,' said Rosa, clicking her teeth in disapproval, though she'd suggested Bertha do the same only yesterday.

'A fool and his money are soon parted,' her mother snapped. 'And that man has been a complete and utter donkey.'

During that afternoon, something very unsettling happened. The ship had raised anchor and left Queenstown, and Bertha's mother and some of the other ladies decided to take afternoon tea in the 2nd Class Library. Bertha had to be dragged along, furious at the prospect of being bored half to death when there was still so much exploring to be done. It was a massive relief to see that she wasn't the only child present. There was another girl in the room: small, with dark hair, bright blue eyes and a dusting of freckles on her nose, standing beside a young woman, who was clutching a chair back for support, and looked pale as death. Bertha's mother, who seemed to be having no trouble at all making friends, made the introductions.

'Robertha, dear, this is Mrs Collyer and her daughter, Marjorie. Poor Mrs Collyer is feeling terribly seasick and is not going to stay for tea after all. Perhaps you and Marjorie could keep each other company.'

Bertha tried to shake hands, but Marjorie wouldn't let go of the large china doll clasped in her arms. The two girls eyed each other warily. To Bertha, Marjorie seemed too young to be of much interest; only eight or nine. But on the other hand, there wasn't a surfeit of suitable companions on the ship. There may have been plenty of twelve-year-old girls in 3rd Class, but they were cut off from her, by the vigilant stewards and the waist high gates barring them from entering the 1st and 2nd Class areas.

'You can call me Madge if you like,' said the girl, putting the doll down carefully on a chair.

'And this is Dolly. Is that an autograph book? Please can I sign it?'

'You can call me Bertha. And yes you can sign, or write a verse or do a drawing, if you'd prefer. But only on one page, if you don't mind. A lot of the passengers haven't had their chance to sign yet.'

Bertha smiled at Madge, a wide, friendly smile, before she realised her mistake and put up her hand to cover her mouth. Madge smiled back. Fortunately, she didn't appear to have noticed anything amiss with Bertha's teeth and just held out her hands to take the book. Bertha handed it over, and decided that Madge would do nicely as a friend, after all.

She was turning the pages of the book, showing her signature collection to Madge, when Ellen Toomey announced that she had a party trick.

'At home in Ireland, I'm considered an expert at reading tea leaves. I told my sister Mary Ann her fourth baby would be a boy, and I was right. If any of you ladies would like their fortune told, I'll be happy to look in your tea cups.'

Bertha's ears pricked up and she snapped the book shut. She'd dismissed Ellen as hopelessly unromantic, but this was riveting. If only she'd been allowed a cup of tea, instead of blackcurrant cordial, Ellen could have read her fortune, and told her which of her million dreams were going to come true. Maybe Ellen would offer to read her mother's, although Bertha could tell by the arched eyebrow and stiff posture that her mother viewed tea leaf reading as superstitious nonsense.

She pulled Madge over to the circle of chairs and leaned in to get a better look. Rosa Pinsky had got in first, and was holding out her cup and saucer.

'Oh read mine, please do!' she giggled.

Ellen gave a gracious nod and issued her instructions.

'First, hold the cup in your left hand, facing your heart. Yes, right there. Now, swirl the tea, three times to the left and finish at your heart.'

Rosa did exactly as she was told, circling her cup in an anti-clockwise direction, so the inch of brown liquid sloshed up the sides. Madge took the opportunity to sneak a shortbread finger, while Bertha leaned in, heart beating fast.

'Upturn the tea into the saucer, and then give the cup to me, so that I can read the leaves.'

Still giggling, Rosa Pinsky handed over her bone china cup.

'What does my future hold? Please tell me I'm about

to receive untold riches!'

The other women laughed.

'Wait and see. My psychic powers are strong, but I need complete silence.'

Ellen was trying hard to seem mysterious, though her efforts were rather hampered by the dollop of cream on her chin, from one of the chocolate éclairs she'd gobbled earlier.

She took the cup, turning it slowly in her hands. For a long moment, she stared at its contents, while everyone waited. Bertha's hands were clasped tight in anticipation. Even Madge was interested now, and was watching, eyes round, velvet hat askew, while Ellen gazed in silence at the smattering of tea leaves in the cup.

Then Ellen finally spoke. Her voice was strained, anxious; her attempt at sounding spooky and mysterious abandoned.

'This has never happened before. It's very peculiar.'

Bertha leaned in further, trying to see if the leaves were placed in some obvious pattern, or were spelling out a message, but Ellen's head was bent low over the cup, and all Bertha could see were the artificial cherries on her felt hat.

'Well?' said Rosa, in a worried tone. 'What can you see?'

'Nothing.'

Ellen Toomey placed the cup on a tray, her hands

trembling. 'It's as if there's a big black wall, and nothing beyond.'

Rosa Pinsky gasped. She looked as if she might be about to cry. Madge's bottom lip wobbled, and Bertha put an arm round the younger girl's shoulders. The air in the room seemed to have turned several degrees colder. There was a long, terrible silence, as everyone in the room wondered what disaster lay ahead.

Chapter 4

Bertha

11th April 1912

Bertha's mother broke the silence with a hearty laugh.

'The sea air is obviously interfering with your psychic powers, Ellen! Perhaps they will return when we're back on dry land. Personally, I can hardly wait to reach America. This ship is built for comfort, not for speed. I would rather be on a faster, more efficient craft!'

It was if she'd waved a magic wand, or broken the wicked fairy's spell. Shoulders relaxed, smiles returned to faces. The adults' conversation veered to matters of transport, with Kate Buss expounding on the benefits of train travel and Marion Wright saying she had read that a female aviator named Harriet Quimby was going to attempt to fly across the English Channel later in the week. Bertha added "*becoming an aviator*" onto her mental list of Things to Achieve in the United Stated of America. Madge pretended to be an actual airplane, swooping and looping-the-loop round the table.

'You two girls could do with some fresh air,' said Mother, catching Madge by the hand. 'Bertha, take

Marjorie out to the Promenade Deck. I am going to retire to the cabin to read for a while and I imagine Mrs Collyer will not be leaving hers again today. She looked very poorly.'

'She has consumption,' said Madge, snatching up her doll, and gripping it so tightly that her fingers turned white. 'That's why we are going to Idaho. Papa says the climate will cure her.'

'Off you go and play, girls.' Mother's voice was brisk, but as she turned away Bertha noticed that her eyes had filled with tears.

After a dozen games of marbles and quoits on the Promenade Deck, Bertha started to feel chilled and decided she and Madge should return the Library. Mother and her friends were long gone, but several other ladies were in there, sipping tea and chatting. They eyed the children disapprovingly, so Bertha abandoned her original plan for races around the room's white fluted columns and ushered Madge over to one of the writing desks by the windows.

Madge wrinkled her nose.

'This place isn't much fun, Bertha. Why don't we go back outside and have a game of hide and seek. Or we could play dolls?'

Bertha gave her a withering stare.

'We have a singular doll. And anyway, I am far too old to play with children's toys.'

Searching for inspiration, her eyes drifted across the desk, and lit on a magnifying glass abandoned on an open book. She snatched it up and waved it in the air.

'I have thought of an excellent ploy!' she declared. 'We shall be detectives. Like Mr Sherlock Holmes and his companion, Watson. I'll be the chief detective, since I have the magnifying glass and can search for significant clues. You can be my faithful helper.'

Madge's bottom lip pouted. She didn't look too happy with this arrangement, but Bertha was adamant. It was her idea after all and she was the elder by four years, which ought to make her leader by default.

All the same, if she couldn't get Madge on side, she'd be playing detective on her own, which she could see wouldn't be fun for long.

'We'll call it *The Collyer-Watt Detective Agency*.'

A half-smile appeared on Madge's face, so Bertha kept going. 'I expect that if we manage to solve any mysteries, we'll be front page news!'

She swept up a copy of today's Atlantic Daily Bulletin and shoved it under Madge's nose.

Madge's face glowed at the prospect of fame. She smoothed her dress, straightened her hat and raked a hand through her dark ringlets, as if expecting a photographer to leap from behind a pillar.

'So what mysteries shall we solve?'

Bertha had been anticipating this question and had

an answer ready. She lowered her voice, trying to make her words sound spooky and mysterious, the way Ellen Toomey did when she was reading the teacup.

'We will know when we find them... stolen goods, dead bodies...'

Wide-eyed, Madge hugged her doll, revelling in the drama. Thoroughly enjoying herself now, Bertha put the magnifying glass to her eye and scanned the room.

'Let's go and find a mystery to solve!'

But then the gong sounded, signalling dinner. Bertha scowled. She didn't like being interrupted mid-idea, and she didn't approve of the dinner gong. It was too similar to the one at home. In 1st Class, a bugle announced dinner, which seemed much more exotic.

Madge sighed.

'I need to go. We shall be eating in the cabin, I expect, if Mum isn't feeling well. See you tomorrow.'

The younger girl skipped off to find her parents. Glancing around, to check she wasn't being observed by anyone who might object to the theft, Bertha slipped the magnifying glass into the deep pocket of her coat, and headed for the Dining Saloon, entirely unaware that a mystery was awaiting her there.

The 2nd Class Dining Saloon was situated aft on D-Deck

and if they hadn't been given that guided tour of the 1st Class facilities, including the very smart Dining Room and Parisian Café yesterday, Bertha was convinced her mother would have thought it supremely elegant. But having seen the lit leaded glass windows, intimate small tables and comfortable armchairs in 1st Class, Mother found the long tables "*not conducive to private conversation*" and was irritated beyond measure by the mahogany swivel chairs.

'Why bolt them to the floor, for goodness' sake?' she complained at every meal. 'It makes it impossible to get comfortably placed at table. And if the weather were to turn so stormy that the chairs went spinning across the floor, I doubt any of us would have the appetite for a three-course meal.'

Bertha, on the other hand, thanked her lucky stars she didn't have to sit through the seven- course meals served in 1st Class. Three courses, plus coffee, were torture enough. The food was delicious, particularly the puddings, but if Bertha had had her way, eating it would have been accomplished in half the time.

Her feet dragged as she reached the entrance, where her mother was waiting, chatting to Marion Wright, whom they'd met yesterday. Bertha heard her mother mention flower arrangements and rolled her eyes behind their backs. Marion was sailing to America to marry her fruit farmer fiancé and Bertha didn't relish the prospect of another ninety minutes of conversation about weddings. She tugged the sleeve of Marion's jacket.

'Why don't you have fireworks instead of flowers at your wedding?' Bertha suggested helpfully. 'They would be so much more entertaining for the guests.' 'That's a charming idea, Bertha, and one I shall definitely consider.' Marion gave her a bright smile and turned back to her mother. 'I'm not even sure which flowers are in season over there!'

The steward took their coats and the women strolled into the dining room, Bertha lagging behind, abandoning all hope of diverting the two women from the most boring topic of conversation in the history of the world.

'What about a simple bouquet of lily of the valley?' Bertha's mother suggested. 'They are so delicate and their scent is delicious.'

Bertha gave a heavy sigh. If only the Collyers had come for luncheon, she could have sat next to Madge, and they could have discussed more important matters, like:

A. *How are we going to get the fingerprints of suspects?*
B. *Where will record all our cases?*
C. *How much should we charge for our services?*

She jumped, startled out of her list making, when

Marion gave a little gasp, and swerved away from their usual table.

'Oh Bessie, there's poor Mr Hoffman. I met him earlier and must introduce you.'

She took Bertha's mother's arm and they glided over to where a handsome, dark-haired man sat, glowering behind a handlebar moustache. Bertha followed, wondering why Marion had described him as "*poor Mr Hoffman*". The adjective hinted at a dark, tragic past, or serious financial difficulties. The tragic past would be so much more interesting.

Please let it be that, she murmured under her breath.

Mr Hoffman stood up as they approached, and smiled, pleasantly enough, but Bertha noticed the way his eyes darted to the door, as if he was anxious to escape.

'This is Mr Louis Hoffman,' declared Marion brightly, oblivious to Mr Hoffman's discomfort. 'And these gorgeous creatures are his little boys, Lolo and Momon. Aren't they just adorable? Do you mind if we join you, Mr Hoffman?'

Mr Hoffman's expression suggested that he couldn't imagine anything more ghastly, but he nodded. His two curly-haired boys gazed, wide-eyed and serious, at them as they sat down, Mother grumbling as her chair swivelled a little too fast. Even Bertha, who was not generally fond of small children, had to agree that the boys *were* adorable.

'We must leave a space for your wife,' said Mother, looking round. 'Will she not be joining us for dinner?'

Marion put a warning hand on Mother's arm.

'Poor Mr Hoffman is widowed, Bess,' she whispered. 'These little ones have lost their Mama.'

Her mother's hand flew to her face.

'Oh, gracious! I'm so sorry to hear that, Mr Hoffman.' She patted the younger boy's fair curls. 'Poor wee souls. Your dear wife must have been so young when she passed. Was she ill long?'

Mr Hoffman seemed to find his cutlery fascinating, he stared at it so hard.

'No. It was very sudden,' he mumbled. 'She died just over a year ago. Her heart...'

'How terribly tragic.'

Mr Hoffman nodded. He picked up a bread roll from a silver plate, and chewed on it, clearly wishing himself elsewhere.

Bertha smiled kindly at the boys, feeling sorry for the poor little mites. She took care not to show her teeth when she smiled, as she knew to her cost that small children could be rather outspoken about them. In London, her wee cousin Phyllis had announced in front of everyone that Bertha had the squintiest teeth she'd ever seen on a person. It had been extremely hurtful and embarrassing.

The little boys didn't smile back, they just gazed at her with their huge, sad eyes.

Bertha was about to speak to them when Mr Hoffman coughed loudly, spraying crumbs.

'My children speak no English, only French. Do not attempt to converse with them. If there's anything you want to say to them, I will translate.'

Mother beamed.

'Oh, my Bertha knows a little French, don't you dear? She learned it at school.'

Mr Hoffman's reaction was mystifying. His face went ashen. His eyes flicked towards the door, and he put a hand on Lolo's shoulder, as if he was about to snatch him up and make a run for it.

'No, no,' he said, a tremble in his voice. 'It is better for them if I translate.'

A current of excitement shot up Bertha's spine. This man was acting very suspiciously. It was crystal clear that he didn't want her to talk to his sons. Something very peculiar was going on, but she couldn't imagine what. It was clearly a case for *The Collyer-Watt Detective Agency*. If only Madge were here to assist!

To get Lolo's attention, she pulled a funny face and stuck out her tongue. He found this as hilarious as she'd hoped, giggling so much he almost fell off his chair. Next, she decided to try out her French. It seemed the only way to get to the bottom of this mystery.

'*La* ...um... *bateau est très*... big... *n'est pas*?'

Lolo stopped giggling. His head cocked.

37

'*Pardon*?'

For some reason this exchange pleased Mr Hoffman greatly. He laughed, so rudely that Bertha felt her cheeks flush as fiery-red as the upholstery.

'As I feared, my son is unable to understand your poor French. Allow me.'

He turned to his older son.

'*C'est un très gros navire, n'est-ce pas?*'

Lolo nodded, his dark curls bouncing. '*Oui, Papa. C'est énorme.*'

Bertha glowered at Mr Hoffman, and considered telling him that he had breadcrumbs lodged in his stupid moustache.

'I understood both of you,' she retorted. 'You said "*isn't the ship enormous*", and Lolo agreed. So, you're quite wrong, my French isn't poor at all. It's perfectly adequate.'

Mother gave Bertha *The Look*, in another futile attempt to remind her that at the dinner table, children should be seen, and not heard. Bertha glared right back.

Mr Hoffman was rude. I was only pointing out the facts.

When their pea soup arrived, everyone tucked in, but Bertha kept a watchful eye on Mr Hoffman, and listened for clues. None materialised. Whatever the man was up to, he wasn't about to confess all at the dinner table. Whenever one of the ladies tried to engage him in conversation, Mr Hoffman's replies were mumbled and evasive, and his eyes kept drifting towards the door.

Bertha had a bad feeling that the Hoffman family would be taking meals in their cabin for the rest of the voyage. She didn't attempt any more French, although when the little boys spoke to one another, she tried hard to work out what they were saying. It seemed to be all about the food. They didn't like the soup, but thought the ice-cream was yummy.

After a while, she gave up and focused on finishing her mental list of Important Matters Pertaining to *The Collyer-Watt Detective Agency*.

D. Should we have a secret password?
E. When we apprehend a suspect, how do we go about making a Citizen's Arrest?

She stopped at E, because it was becoming tricky to keep all the *Important Matters* in her head. A casebook was going to be essential.

After dinner, while the ladies went for an evening stroll on the Promenade Deck, Bertha slipped back to the cabin and got out her precious burgundy leather autograph book. It was a going away present from her school friends, who'd written "*Good Luck*" and "*Bon Voyage*" and "*I'll miss you so much*" messages on the first few pages.

On her first day aboard ship, Bertha had stuck her book under the noses of as many passengers and crew as she could, and they'd all seemed pleased to be asked to contribute a signature or a little verse. Kind Mr Weisz had done a beautiful drawing of a flower in it. Even the Captain had signed, and Mr Andrews, the ship's designer, who'd told her while signing that he had a daughter called Elba, named after her initials, Elizabeth Law Barbour Andrews.

Bertha sighed wistfully, running her fingers over the embossed initials on the cover of her book... *RJW*. If only her parents had thought harder about her name. There was no way of making a pretty nickname from *Robertha Josephine Watt*.

She skimmed through the pages, reading the signatures, while worrying that perhaps she'd been a bit hasty in allowing so many people to add their names. But luckily, there were plenty of blank pages left to log the activities of *The Collyer-Watt Detective Agency*.

Hand trembling with excitement, she wrote the date, and then set out the facts of the case: *The Mystery of Mr Louis Hoffman.*

Clue 1: *Mr Hoffman has shifty eyes.*

Clue 2: *The little boys seem worried and anxious.*

Clue 3: *Mr Hoffman does not want people to talk to them in their own language.*

Possible Solutions:

A. Mr Hoffman is an evil kidnapper and has taken the children from their rightful parents.
B. He treats the children cruelly and does not want his cruelty to be discovered.
C. The boys are sad because their mother has died, and he wants to protect them from having to talk to strangers.

She shut the book, tingling with excitement, looking forward to telling Madge all about it in the morning. But the next morning something so strange happened, that *The Mystery of Mr Hoffman* almost faded from Bertha's mind.

Chapter 5

Johan

12th of April 1912

The first couple of days of the voyage were undiluted misery for Johan. To his cabin mates' obvious disgust, he spent the time being violently seasick, throwing up into a tin bowl and once, to his shame, in the cabin's shared enamel sink, where he'd retched while trying to clean vomit from his hair.

'Oi!'

The voice from the top bunk had been so lacking in sympathy that the pain of missing his mother had felt sharper than the ache in his guts.

'Don't puke in there, you dirty beggar! We paid extra to get that sink!'

Svinpäls.

Nobody had ever called him such a name before. Johan had thrown him himself back on his bunk, and wished himself dead. This trip had been torture from the beginning. At least on the boat to Hull he'd been out on deck, leaning over the railings to spew into the choppy waters of the North Sea. Down here, in this windowless, stuffy cabin, he longed for fresh air, a cooling breeze. But every time he tried to get up, the motion of the ship and the constant throb of its engines made him feel so dizzy he had to lie down again.

The three others in the cabin were all Swedish lads, older than him, intent on having a good time, and reluctant to be saddled with an ill, miserable, boy. They visited the 3rd Class Common Room in the evenings, bowling out clutching beer bottles, a fiddle and an accordion box, and didn't return to the cabin until the early hours, singing bawdy songs, and crashing around in the dark, oblivious to Johan's presence.

But early in the morning of the 12th, Johan was lying on his bunk, groaning and listless, when the door opened and one of the lads entered, a tin cup in his hand. Steam drifted from the cup like smoke from a ship's funnel. The lad held the cup in front of Johan, a kind smile on his handsome face.

'Here, lad. Drink this. It'll make you feel better.'

Tears brimmed in Johan's eyes, and he wiped them away, ashamed. What was it about this ship? Since boarding, he'd been constantly crying or on the verge of tears.

The dark-haired lad tried again. 'Come on, now. Sit yourself up and drink this. Titanic's best beef tea. According to the steward I asked, it's the best remedy for sea sickness. And I've a cabin biscuit in my pocket for you too.'

Johan shook his head. A rich, meaty smell was emanating from the cup, and it was making his guts twist. But the young man was determined. He helped Johan into a sitting position and handed him the cup, which he almost dropped, the handle was so hot. Then he plonked himself down on the opposite bunk and watched, as the boy sipped the steaming brown gruel, and tried not to gag.

'There you go! Get that down you, and keep it down. Here's the biscuit. I'm Nils, by the way. I'm heading for Illinois to study agriculture. My uncle lives there and bought me the ticket. You?'

'Johan Cervin Svensson.' He took a gulp of beef tea, burning his tongue. 'I'm going to Clay County, South Dakota, to work on my father's farm—if I don't die of seasickness before I get there.'

Nils studied Johan, his brown eyes warm and sympathetic.

'I felt the same, the first time my uncle took me out on his fishing boat. I spent the whole trip puking over the side and, like you, I thought I was dying. You'll get used to the movement of the ship soon. It's worse down here on the lower decks, but she's very smooth compared to some. Once you're up and about, you'll feel like a new man.'

He smiled again, his dark eyes crinkling. 'You've been

so out of it you've missed the stops at Cherbourg and Queenstown. We're steaming across the Atlantic now and are forecast to reach New York in another 5 days, so not long now!'

'Maybe he should have got off in Queenstown, eh? Given us all peace from his retching,' growled a voice from the top bunk. A face loomed, twisted in a gargoyle-like sneer.

Nils scowled.

'Aw, lay off, Oskar. Leave him alone. He's only a young lad.'

Johan drank the rest of the beef tea, nibbled the dry biscuit, and lay back on his bunk. He could feel strength seeping back into his limbs. The horrible head spinning, stomach churning sickness was starting to fade. And as his strength returned, two things dawned on him. First, that he had eaten nothing but that biscuit for two whole days, and was absolutely ravenous. Secondly, he hadn't checked on his property since the ship had sailed out of Southampton Water. When he leaned over the bunk, he could see the corner of his bag peeking out, still safely stashed. His ticket was in there.

It had come from his father, along with a long letter, telling him that times were hard, even in America, and warning him that he'd better be prepared to work his fingers to the bone when he reached the farm in South Dakota. His father hadn't made the prospect of life in

America sound remotely appealing... it sounded much like his life in Sweden basically, but with burning sun and rattlesnakes.

When he'd handed his ticket over on boarding, the purser had torn off a section, kept it and given him back the rest. He'd stuffed it in the bottom of his bag, along with a spare shirt, two pairs of mittens his mother had knitted for Jenny and Pa, and his Inspection Card.

The map wasn't in the bag. It had been in his trouser pocket, and his trousers were draped over the end of the bunk. His jacket was hanging on a peg screwed to the cabin door.

What if someone's rifled my pockets while I've been ill? I wouldn't put it past that one in the top bunk.

But when he sat up, and tugged his trousers towards him, he heard the faint rustle of paper. The map was still there. After an initial rush of relief, he began to worry. Time was running out. The map had lain in his pocket for two whole days, and he'd done nothing about it. He was no nearer to discovering its secret, and there were only a few days left before this ship reached land.

While the others got washed and dressed, which involved a lot of noisy shoving and laughing, and squeezing past each other in the tight confines of the cabin, Johan pulled the blanket over his head, and pretended to go back to sleep. He was glad he was in a cabin with fellow Swedes, as at least he understood what they were saying, but he didn't feel it was possible for him to join in their banter. Two days of throwing up had ruined any chance of making a good impression. Anyway, what was the point of trying to make friends? Once in America, his life on the farm would be a mind-numbing grind of work-sleep-work. There would be no time for friendship—or a social life.

When the bell sounded, and Nils and the others left to get breakfast, Johan heaved a sigh of relief, pulled on his clothes, checked that the key was safe in his jacket pocket, and then lay on his bunk, enjoying the quiet for a little longer. It seemed prudent to wait until the next seating, as he was keen to sit alone, away from the others. He needed peace to think about the map. Should he ask Nils to take a look at it? He seemed kind, and if he was studying, there was a chance he could read English, but how could he trust him not to tell the others?

Johan left the cabin, and used gestures to get directions to the Dining Saloon. On his way, he kept an eye out for the red-haired man, but as he headed along the corridor, which seemed to stretch from one end of the ship to the other, there was no sign of him. Of course, he'd give both the key and the letter back to the man if asked, but he'd much prefer not to be asked.

When Johan reached the Dining Saloon, he scanned the room, but none of the diners had bright red hair. He handed his table ticket to a steward, who gave him a postcard, with what he guessed was a menu. The table ticket had been partly in Swedish, but the menu was indecipherable. Maybe it would have been better to eat with the other Swedish lads. How was he meant to know what to ask for? He glanced around, blinking nervously. The room was gleaming white, brightly lit by sidelights. Even the tables were white, covered with crisp Irish linen tablecloths. It was spotless, but it wasn't what he'd call homely.

Johan was directed to his space at one of the long tables, and sat down, surrounded by young men talking in a dozen different languages. The morning meal was served by uniformed stewards; by sweeping his hand the length of the postcard, he asked for everything. There was oatmeal porridge, smoked herrings, jacket potatoes, freshly baked Swedish bread and marmalade.

He never had so much to eat at home and felt stuffed and drowsy by the end of the meal, but he had no desire to return to the cabin, so instead slipped out of the Dining Saloon and headed up the stairs.

Somehow, he needed to find a stranger; one who could read English and hopefully speak Swedish and who would agree to translate the words on the map, and then leave him alone and show no further interest in the matter.

Johan had managed to convince himself that this piece of paper was the answer to his prayers. If there was money hidden somewhere on this ship, he was going to find it and change the course of his life. He didn't want to be a farm labourer all his life. He wanted to build ships and motor cars but what were the chances of that? The way things were, his father would never let him leave the farm. And there would never be enough money for the rest of his family to come to America too.

He straightened his tie, buttoned his jacket, figuring that he looked smart enough to pass for a 2nd Class passenger, and just as long as he strolled in a casual manner, and didn't act guilty or subservient, he should get away with it. The difficulty now was how to access the 2nd Class areas?

First, he headed up to the Poop Deck, which was crowded with children, who were running between the storage areas, ducking under the cranes, and leaping from benches, while their mothers sat gossiping, enjoying the fresh air. But there were steps and a rail barring the way to the other areas of the Boat Deck, and a steward standing by it.

This wasn't going to be as easy as he'd thought. On the other hand, the actual physical barriers wouldn't be a bother. He had plenty of experience of scrambling over walls or shimmying under fences back in Sweden, while poaching rabbits or stealing apples from the neighbouring orchard.

The system of segregation was only working on this

ship because everybody was sticking to the rules, staying obediently in their designated areas. Johan's next move was clear: he would need to break their stupid rules.

Chapter 6

Bertha

12th April 1912

Bertha was sitting, bouncing with impatience, on a bench on the Promenade Deck, her treasured autograph book on her lap. She was waiting for Madge, who hadn't appeared in the Dining Saloon at breakfast time, and was desperate to tell her all about the mysterious Mr Hoffman.

And then she noticed a boy, leaning against the nearest funnel stack. At first she thought he was snoozing, but then realised that he was staring at her, so directly it made her feel uncomfortable. He looked out of place, in his scruffy clothes and worn boots, and she shifted uneasily on the bench, and looked around to see if she could see Madge. But when she turned back, the boy was still there, head cocked as if he was considering something.

He seemed to make up his mind and strolled over, took off his cap and gave her a stiff little bow.

'Excuse me,' he said. '*Talar froken svenska?*'

Up close, she could see he was younger than she'd

thought, not much older than she was. He had vivid blue eyes, startling blond hair and when he smiled, enviably even white teeth.

'I am sorry, but I cannot understand what you are saying,' said Bertha. He didn't reply, so she thought she had better explain further. 'I speak English, although I am actually Scottish. I am from a city called Aberdeen in Scotland. Do you know it? It's quite far north and is famous for its granite buildings. It's actually known as the Granite City...'

She stopped talking, because the boy was gawping at her. Perhaps he'd never heard of Aberdeen, or didn't speak any English at all. Maybe he wasn't the full shilling. There was a long, awkward silence, and Bertha began to wish her mother was with her, and not in the Library writing letters. Her mother always seemed to know how to fill in gaps in conversation.

Then the boy's smile lit his face again, and she figured he'd decided she was friend, rather than foe. He rummaged in his trouser pocket and drew out a crumpled scrap of paper, which he handed to her, carefully, as though it were precious.

'Excuse me.'

She took the paper, and turned it over in her hands; it was stained and dirty, but she tried not to show her distaste.

'What do you want me to do with it?' asked Bertha.

He didn't answer, but he seemed to be waiting, head still cocked to the side, like a curious robin.

One side of the paper was scrawled with loopy, untidy handwriting. Bertha scanned it, her head whirling. What on earth was going on? Perhaps the boy wanted her to read this letter aloud to him, but why, when he didn't appear to understand English? She glanced up at him, and he gave her an encouraging smile. This time she wasn't taken in by the gleam of his beautiful teeth. She noticed that despite the smile, there was no warmth in his eyes. There was wariness there, and suspicion. He didn't trust her any further than she trusted him.

'This side is a letter,' she said, showing him. 'It is written in English. I can read it to you, if you like?'

She'd accompanied her words with a mime, pretending to read, her eyes moving from left to right down a page, as if she were playing a game of charades. It seemed to work, as the boy nodded, and sat down by her side. Embarrassed, she shifted fractionally along the bench.

When she'd asked why there were locked gates on the ship, a steward had told her the passengers were kept apart because of American immigration laws. The 3rd Class passengers needed to be health checked on arrival at Ellis Island in New York; in case any were infected by lice or disease. Her mother would not be pleased if she came back to the cabin with head lice. And the boy smelled strangely of Bovril. Although, under torture,

Bertha would have had to confess that she didn't move because of hygiene concerns. She'd just never sat so close to a similarly aged boy before, and found the experience faintly disturbing.

'*Dear George*,' she began, speaking in a loud, clear voice, which she hoped could be understood by anyone, of any nationality.

'*As I told you at Alice's funeral last month, I worked as a riveter on the very ship you've been taken on as a stoker. You will understand that I was not in the right frame of mind to talk about this matter at the funeral. Emily and I were both heartbroken, and still are. Alice was the light of our lives, and the light has been snuffed out.*

I am writing you now, as I need your help. One of the riveters on my team was a thieving bug...'

Bertha paused half way through the word and blushed a fiery red. Swearing didn't come as naturally as she'd hoped.

'*Was a... thief, so while I was on the ship, I kept my treasures in a little locked box. As you know, Emily, Alice and me took sick with the typhus fever and I never got back on the Titanic to retrieve my property, before the ship left Belfast. I have enclosed the key for the lock and if you could fetch my treasures and post them home to me, I would be forever grateful.*

Safe travels,

Your cousin, Francis.

Bertha turned the letter over, and then faced the boy, her face glowing with excitement.

'The man who wrote this letter, Francis somebody, has hidden treasure somewhere on this ship! We must find it for him! Do you have the key he mentions in his letter?'

The boy's face looked utterly blank and it dawned on Bertha that he didn't have a clue what she was talking about. Perhaps he hadn't understood her loud, clear tones as well as she'd hoped.

She waved the letter in front of his face, to indicate she was talking about its contents.

'A man hid something...' She did another little mime, pretending to pick up an imaginary object and hide it under her coat. The boy nodded, seeming to understand. 'He hid silver, or gold, or diamonds on the ship.'

She pointed at the silver bracelet on her wrist, a farewell gift from her father.

'And this,' she added, waving the paper again. 'This is an actual treasure map!'

The boy's pale face glowed. Tears sparkled, sapphire-blue, in his eyes.

'*Det ar en skattkarta*?'

'*Skattkarta*. Yes, I think so... if that word means treasure map.'

She glanced from the boy to the letter and back, and then rubbed at her nose, puzzled. He didn't look old enough or strong enough to be working as a stoker.

'Is this your letter?'

He shrugged, not seeming to understand, so she tried again, with lots of pointing.

'My name is Robertha Josephine Watt. Is your name George?'

The boy shook his head, and jabbed at his chest with a grimy finger.

'Johan Cervin Svensson.'

Then he mimed dropping an object, and catching it.

'*Han kastade den.*'

Bertha watched, struggling to work out if the boy had found the letter or stolen it. She decided it didn't much matter, figuring she could hardly get judgemental when a stolen magnifying class was weighing down her pocket.

Struggling to contain her excitement, Bertha wrapped her arms around herself.

'Oh, I do believe this is another case for *The Collyer-Watt Detective Agency*!'

Hidden treasure... a treasure map... kidnapped children... Wait until Madge hears about all this!

And then, to her delight, she saw her friend in the distance, skipping along the Promenade Deck, the china doll in her arms, accompanied by a tall, balding man in a dark suit. The boy saw them coming, and snatched the paper out of Bertha's hand. Aghast at the thought of losing the Detective Agency's newest case, Bertha tried to grab it back.

'Wait here! You'll need our help to find the treasure, won't you?'

But the boy was having none of that, and stuffed the treasure map in his trouser pocket, where it was utterly irretrievable.

Bertha thought he was going to run off, and the adventure was going to be over before it had properly begun, but he stood in front of her, and pointed at the bench.

'*Jag kommer tillbaka.*'

He held up ten fingers. She nodded, hoping he meant he'd meet her there at ten o'clock tomorrow, because there was no time to clarify the arrangements before he scuttled off.

Bertha pulled the autograph album on to her lap, and by the time Madge arrived, she was scribbling feverishly with one of her father's graphite pencils, recording all the details of *The Case of the Strange Boy and the Treasure Map*.

'Bertha, this is my Daddy.'

Bertha snapped the book shut, stood up and shook hands with Harvey Collyer, who seemed gratifyingly delighted that Madge had found a suitable friend.

'Splendid. Aberdeen, you say? I've never been to Scotland, but I've heard it's ever so scenic. Keep your coat buttoned, Madge. There's a chill in the air, and we can't have you catching a cold.'

Mr Collyer walked off to continue his promenade along the deck, leaving them alone on the bench.

'Poor Daddy,' sighed Madge. 'He's always worrying about my health, and he hardly gets out of the cabin, as Mum needs him.'

She placed the doll down beside her on the bench.

'What were you writing about?'

Heart thumping with excitement, Bertha opened the book and read *The Collyer-Watt Detective Agency's* case notes, including her brand new, hastily written notes on *Case 2: The Strange Boy and the Treasure Map:*

Clue 1: *The mysterious letter. Real or forgery? Is there anybody on board who does handwriting analysis?*
Clue 2: *The foreign boy... clearly from Scandinavia, as very blond. Does Svenka mean Sweden? (Check with Mother.)*
Clue 3: *The treasure map. Real or forgery?*

Possible Solutions:

A. *The strange boy is playing a mean trick.*
B. *There is treasure hidden in the cargo hold!*

By the time she'd finished reading, Madge was trembling with excitement, hugging her doll close.

'Oh, my goodness! This is such a fun game!'

Bertha gave her a hard stare. 'The Detective Agency isn't a game, Madge. It is deadly serious. Lives are at stake.'

Madge tried to pull her face into the required expression, but she didn't look terribly convinced.

'There is nothing we can do about the second case until we meet the boy tomorrow at ten o'clock,' said Bertha, snapping the book shut. 'So we should work on the first case today. Let's see if we can solve *The Mystery of Mr Hoffman*.'

Madge nodded, her eyes sparkling. Bertha fished the magnifying glass out of her pocket, waving it in the air like a magic wand.

'Now that our plans are laid, let's go and find some more clues!'

She stuffed the magnifying glass back in her pocket, tucked the autograph book under her arm and they set off to find the mysterious Mr Hoffman.

Chapter 7

Bertha

12th April 1912

First, they searched the entire length of the 2nd Class Promenade Deck, walking past a group of middle aged ladies huddled in their hired deckchairs, three small boys playing quoits, and an elderly couple strolling arm in arm. The Promenade Deck reminded Bertha of the Esplanade at Aberdeen Beach. The sea breeze was just as frigid, and she expected the churning water below would be equally icy; thank goodness there was no chance of finding out.

'The Hoffmans definitely aren't here,' said Madge, already sounding deflated. 'Maybe they're spending the whole day in their cabin. We could have a tea party for Dolly instead, if you like.'

Bertha shook her head.

'You mustn't give up so easily, Madge. Detectives have to be intelligent and observant, but they must also have a dogged determination to solve the most difficult of cases. Let's think about this rationally. Mr Hoffman would go crazy—if he isn't a certified lunatic already—

trapped in a cabin all day with two small, energetic boys. Let's try C-Deck.'

She opened the door of the little deckhouse and they trooped inside. It was a relief to be free of the biting wind. Bertha wanted to take the elevator down, as she thought Reginald, the lift-boy, was very handsome, and he was always happy to chat, and who wouldn't be, trapped in a lift all day and night? But Madge announced she was afraid of the jolts, and petrified that the cables would break and they'd plummet to the bottom, so instead they clattered down the stairs to C-Deck. Its long, enclosed promenade was so like the glasshouses in Cruikshank Botanic Gardens; it seemed the perfect place to bring two small boys.

And she was right again! There they were, Mr Hoffman and the two boys, among the mothers and babies and little children spinning tops and playing a rowdy game of tag.

She could see Lolo, his dark curls bouncing, as he jumped up and down, trying to see out of the windows.

'Remember we mustn't do anything to arouse suspicion,' said Bertha, grabbing Madge's arm before she skipped into the play area. 'Don't ask me to produce the magnifying glass in Mr Hoffmann's presence. And if I say anything in French, don't act surprised.'

'How will I know you're speaking French, Bertha?' asked Madge. 'I've never heard anyone speak French before.'

'You'll know because you won't understand what I am saying, but hopefully the boys will.'

'What will you say to them?'

'I will play it by ear.'

Madge looked suitably impressed.

Together, the girls walked towards the Hoffmans; Bertha's heart was beating wildly. Madge was treating *The Collyer-Watt Detective Agency* as a wonderful game of pretend, and she had to admit that had been how it had started, but now they had real cases to solve. There was something peculiar about Mr Hoffman, she could sense it. Perhaps she had supernatural powers, like Ellen Toomey.

As they drew close, Madge tugged at Bertha's sleeve.

'Is that one of the little boys? Oh, he's a sweetheart!'

She veered over to the window to introduce herself to Lolo, so it was only Bertha who saw little Momon leap into Mr Hoffman's arms, put his chubby arms around his neck and give him an affectionate hug. For a long moment, Bertha stood, wondering if she had made a terrible mistake. Today, Mr Hoffman looked the very image of a loving father, and nothing like the evil child stealer she'd imagined him to be yesterday.

'Good morning, Mr Hoffmann. It's a pleasant morning, if a little overcast.'

Bertha had heard her mother say these very words

to Mrs Pinsky earlier, so was confident in their delivery.

'Yes, pleasant enough, though getting chillier, I feel.'

The conversation faltered. Mr Hoffmann looked away, seeming to feel it was over.

Bertha took a deep breath. 'Mr Hoffmann, the girl over there is my friend, Marjorie Collyer. She is English, not Scottish like me, but perfectly respectable. We were wondering if perhaps you would like us to take the boys for a short walk?'

She was watching him closely, noticing his reluctance, and how he gripped Momon tighter. All her suspicions returned. Mr Hoffman seemed locked in a private battle, caught between his desire for some time alone and his wish to stop his children from communicating with others. But the lure of some child-free moments won.

'I could do with a quick visit to the barber's shop,' he said, running his hand along his drooping moustache. 'You may keep my children entertained for ten minutes, but I insist you remain in this area.'

He put Momon down, patted his curls, and looked straight at Bertha, a warning in his eyes.

'There is no need for you to speak to them in French. It will only confuse them.'

At that moment Madge skipped over, followed by Lolo, who was beaming in delight, and clutching Madge's doll.

'*J'ai une poupée, Papa!*' shouted Lolo.

Mr Hoffman laughed and started to walk towards the elevator.

'*Mais les poupées sont pour les filles, Lolo.*'

Lolo's bottom lip wobbled. Tears brimming in his eyes, he handed the doll back to Madge.

If Bertha had been a dog, she'd have growled.

'What a mean, untrue thing to say. My cousins, Jack and Joe, play quite happily with dolls. They call them tin soldiers, but they're dolls, all the same.'

She held the little boy by the shoulders.

'*Les poupées sont aussi pour les garçons.*'

Lolo smiled.

'*Maman dit ça aussi.*'

Bertha leapt back, as if she'd been electrocuted. She grabbed Madge's arm, whispered in her ear.

'I said dolls are also for boys, and Lolo said Mummy says that too. How would he remember, Madge, what his mother told him, if she died over a year ago? He must have been Momon's age, hardly more than a baby. It doesn't make any sense!'

Madge's eyes widened. She was about to reply, but Lolo and Momon were looking at them expectantly, waiting to be entertained, so Bertha shook her head.

'We will discuss the matter later,' she said firmly, and began a game of chase, which ended badly when Momon tripped head first on the deck and started to wail.

Luckily, by the time Mr Hoffmann returned, his sobs

had faded to sniffles, and Lolo seemed disappointed that the girls couldn't stay longer.

'We could come and play with them again tomorrow, if that would be convenient?' said Bertha to Mr Hoffmann, as she tried to disentangle Lolo, who had wrapped his arms around her knees.

'Perhaps.'

Mr Hoffman gave an approximation of a smile, though his newly-waxed moustache barely twitched. '*Lolo, Momon... Venez!*'

He took a child in each hand and together they walked off, heading towards the elevator.

Bertha stared after them, her mind whirling like a Catherine Wheel.

She sat down on a bench and Madge plonked herself down beside her.

'This is a fiendishly difficult case,' Bertha announced, opening her book and pulling her pencil from her pocket. 'The question is, can it be solved by the two brilliant minds of *The Collyer-Watt Detective Agency*?'

'I don't know, Bertha.' Madge glanced up, then went back to tying the sash on her doll's dress. 'To tell the honest truth, I don't exactly know what's going on, but it doesn't matter because I'm having great fun.'

Bertha sighed. Madge was sweet, but she didn't really possess the sharp, incisive brain necessary for a truly great detective.

'Writing down all the clues will help to clarify matters, you'll see.'

Bertha licked the tip of the pencil and began to write.

Clue 4: *Lolo can remember something said by his mother. How can that be?*

Possible Solutions:

A. *Lolo has an exceptional memory for a three-year-old.*
B. *Mr Hoffmann lied about the date of Mrs Hoffmann's death. Could he be involved????*
C. *Mrs Hoffmann is still alive, and for some reason Mr Hoffman is keeping her a secret.*

Perhaps she is insane, and he has locked her in the attic, so that he can remarry, like Mr Rochester does in *Jane Eyre*.

Madge watched as she wrote, and then pointed at Solution B.

'What do you mean, Bertha?'

'I mean, perhaps Mr Hoffmann is responsible for the death of his wife.' Bertha paused, for extra dramatic effect. 'Maybe he is a wife poisoner like Doctor Crippen!'

Madge's eyes were as round as moons.

'I've never heard of Doctor Crippen. Was he a real person, or a story?'

'He was as real as you and me.' Bertha lowered her voice. 'Until he was hanged for his terrible crime.'

She shivered, having managed to scare herself. Two years ago, the Crippen Case had been the talk of the school playground and had given her such nightmares she'd had to sleep with a light on for weeks.

'Dr Crippen tried to escape to America,' she remembered. 'But he was caught aboard the ship!'

She grabbed Madge's hand.

'We need to tell the Captain that Mr Hoffman is a murderer!'

They started running, and were half way to the steps when the luncheon gong sounded.

Boiing!

Bertha skidded to a halt.

'Oh for goodness' sake!' she grumbled. 'Meals on this ship are such an inconvenience. We've just discovered that an evil wife poisoner is on board the Titanic and they've made it impossible for us to go and tell the appropriate authorities.'

She pondered for a moment on whether the Hoffman case was so important she should ignore the gong, but the lure of pudding won.

'Shall we meet here after luncheon?'

Madge shook her head, eyes full of regret.

'Mum, Daddy and I are having a little picnic in the cabin and Mum asked if I would stay and keep her company this afternoon. She's going to teach me how to crochet. I don't suppose you'd mind speaking to the Captain on your own, would you, Bertha? You're terribly brave. I would never be able to march up to a stranger and strike up a conversation the way you can.'

Bertha walked a little taller on her way to the Dining Saloon. Never before had she been described as "*terribly brave*". Already, even before the mystery of Mr Hoffmann had been solved, she felt like a hero.

She was going to rescue these two little boys from the clutches of their evil, wife-poisoning father, and everyone on the ship would hear about it. If the news got into the papers, perhaps her Papa would read about it in the Portland Oregonian. He sent regular snippets of their local news home. Imagine how impressed he would be to see his own daughter in the newspaper!

But first, she had to sit through yet another tedious meal, surrounded by adults, most of whom she hardly knew, while trying very hard not to slurp her soup, or spill the gravy, or gobble her tapioca pudding, or talk too much, in case her mother gave her *The Look*.

Hopefully, in Oregon, it would be different. With any luck, Americans liked children to be both seen and heard at the table, as she was sure she'd explode like an overheated can of condensed milk, if she had to keep her thoughts and opinions to herself for much longer.

Though, on this occasion at least, it was vital that she

kept quiet. Mr Hoffmann mustn't know of her suspicions, before she'd had the chance to tell the Captain everything they'd discovered about his dreadful crime.

Chapter 8

Johan

12th April 1912

It appeared that getting out of the 2nd Class Passenger area, without getting nabbed by a crew member, was going to prove trickier than entering.

Despite Johan's worry, getting in had been a breeze: just a climb up some steps, a quick glance to check nobody was watching, and a vault of the barrier. He'd jinked behind one of the giant funnels and looked around for someone who might be able to help him in his quest. And then he'd seen the girl. She'd been jigging up and down on a bench, just a few yards away, scanning the deck as though she were waiting for someone to arrive. He'd waited, and watched, nodding to himself when he noted the book on her lap: evidence that she could read. Perhaps she's The One, he'd thought. She can read, and she's sitting on her own, so there are no folks to talk her out of helping me or who might call for a steward. Of course, she might shoo me away or yell for a steward herself, but that's a risk I'm going to have to take.

As Johan waited, gathering his courage, he'd tried

to guess the girl's nationality. He'd decided she must be American, probably returning from a holiday or visiting family. She wasn't a migrant, like him, travelling in search of a better life—not in that fur-collared coat and those buttoned boots.

And who was she waiting for, jiggling with such impatience that the book dropped off her lap—twice? It seemed most likely she that she was travelling with her parents, and he couldn't imagine why she was so excited about the prospect of them arriving on the Promenade Deck, when surely she'd seen them at the breakfast table?

For some reason, the thought of the girl eating breakfast with her parents had floored him. His knees had buckled and he'd had to clutch at the funnel for support. He'd needed to take several deep breaths, eyes closed.

I miss my family so much. I want to go home, or I want them here with me. One or the other, but not this. I don't want to be separated from them by three thousand miles of ocean.

He'd tried to picture it, tried to imagine the joy of seeing his mother and brothers and sister appear on deck, heading towards him, calling his name, their arms outstretched. He could picture himself, laughing and joking with them, swinging his youngest brother up into his arms, the others gathered round, hugging him tight. He could hear their warm, familiar voices, see his mother's tear-filled eyes, her joyous smile. And then a terrible thought had crashed over him like a wave. I will never see my mother again.

A chill had spread through his body, as though he'd been thrown in icy water. He'd shivered, trying to shake the thought from his head, but it had turned solid as ice, and would not be moved.

When he'd opened his eyes, it was as if he'd been underwater, and had floated to the surface, gulping for air. It was at that moment he'd realised the girl was staring straight at him.

Get a grip, you idiot. The treasure will fix everything.

He'd straightened his shoulders, and stared right back. And then, having checked again that nobody else was striding across the deck towards her, he'd approached, moving swiftly before the last of his courage seeped away.

Initially, he thought he'd chosen well. The girl hadn't yelled for a steward. She'd been able to read the letter and she'd even seemed to understand its importance. But that bright glint in her eyes, her obvious excitement when she'd realised what she was holding, had worried him, and he hadn't liked the way she'd tried to snatch the map back. He hadn't liked that at all.

He might need the girl's help to read the instructions on the map, but the treasure was his, because his need for it was so much greater. She had wealth and education, the tickets to freedom. But how could he explain that to her, when they didn't speak the same language?

When he'd seen the balding man and the little girl approaching, he'd bolted, but when he'd run past them, he'd seen the man's eyebrows gather, suspicion darkening his eyes. As Johan had darted behind the funnel, it had dawned on him that he didn't look the part after all, and that compared to everyone else in 2nd Class, his clothes were scruffy, his hair unkempt, and he smelled unpleasant. He'd lay bets none of the 2nd Class passengers had been forced to stick out their tongues or have their scalps checked for lice—or have their eyelids pulled back with a button hook.

It was time to leave, before he was collared by a steward.

But while he was up there, the Promenade Deck had got busier, and there seemed to be twice as many crew members as passengers. There were stewards everywhere, unfailingly polite and helpful: bringing steamer rugs and hot drinks to the ladies, setting up and putting away the hired deckchairs. And if they spotted him, he guessed that veneer would rub off, and he'd be cornered, grabbed by the collar and stuck in the hold for the rest of the voyage.

Remembering the medical inspection had made Johan realise something: the 3rd Class passengers were kept separate from the rest—not simply because of they'd bought cheaper tickets—but because the authorities were afraid they'd spread disease.

So, it appeared that he was stuck there, crouching behind a funnel, until he could come up with a better plan than flinging himself over the gate and risking a chase.

An elderly lady shuffled past, a little dog yapping at her heels. She was heading towards a small deckhouse, which presumably covered the stairway to the lower decks. It occurred to Johan that getting back to 3rd Class might be easier from another deck, so he left the funnel and followed the lady. As she reached the deckhouse door, she scooped the dog into her arms and went inside. Johan waited a few seconds before pushing the door open.

To his relief, he found himself at the top of a smart staircase, with polished oak balustrades and red and white patterned linoleum. There was no sign of the old lady, but he jumped, startled, when somebody behind him spoke.

'Do you want to use the lift too, sir?'

A dark-haired, uniformed boy, who was only about sixteen, was standing at a curved, wrought-iron gate. The gate seemed odd, out of place on the ship. When Johan peered through it, he glimpsed the old lady, not in a garden, as he'd half-expected, but standing, dog in her arms, in a tiny, cell-like room. He caught her frown, her narrowed eyes. She knew he didn't belong. The boy seemed oblivious, and was smiling, a wide, friendly grin. He beckoned at Johan to get in beside them, but Johan shook his head, and backed away. Why on earth would he want to enter? He'd be caught like a rat in a trap, locked in that cell and interrogated by the stewards until he was forced to confess that he'd crossed the class divide, risking the health of self-made millionaires and aristocrats alike.

Panicking, he flung himself down the stairs, so fast that his booted feet skidded on the polished linoleum, leaving dirty black marks. When he reached the next landing, a high- pitched bark made him spin round. His jaw dropped, as another gate opened, and the same old woman he'd just seen on the Promenade Deck was guided out of an identical room by the same smiling boy. *Was there a ladder or a spiral staircase in there, or was the box somehow moving up and down?*

It was the weirdest thing he'd ever seen, but he couldn't stay to figure it all out, because the woman shouted, 'Come here, boy!' and although he didn't understand the words, her imperious tone told him he'd been rumbled.

He kept going, but when he reached the bottom of the stairs, he had to admit to himself that he had no idea which deck he was on, nor how to get back to his own quarters. He started walking along a long, straight corridor, past closed doors, some numbered, others with signs, with the letters KEEP OUT and PRIVATE. He began to feel as if he'd entered a labyrinth, from which he'd never escape, doomed to wander forever in this complex maze of corridors and stairways, utterly, hopelessly lost. He came to a set of steps and was about to climb them, when behind him, a voice bellowed.

'Oi, you!'

Johan whirled round and came face to face with a demon from the depths of hell. A hideous creature with red-rimmed eyes, its blackened face contorted with fury.

The creature's filthy hand shot out and grabbed Johan's shoulder, gripping so hard that despite his thick jacket, its nails dug into his skin.

'Give them back, you little swine!' Johan was flung back and forth, shaken like a rag rug on wash day.

He struggled, kicked out, but the monster was far too strong.

'*Lamna mig ifred!*' *Leave me alone*!

'You took the map and the key. Give them back!'

Johan recognised a single word.

Map... Karte.

As he drove a fist towards the creature's face, he saw a tinge of ginger in the soot-blackened hair, and realisation dawned.

The red-haired stoker had him by the collar, and he wanted his property back. The rattling was making it impossible to think rationally, but Johan tried to rummage in his jacket pockets, hoping to find the map. It wasn't worth dying for. But the map wasn't there, and he couldn't work out why. He could feel the key, cold against his fingertips, but it was useless without the map. How could he explain himself to this furious foreigner?

'*Jag har inte dem!*' *I don't have them*!

He shouted, hating the high, panicky sound of his voice. His fists flailed, and he squirmed like an eel in a fishermen's net, but the stoker's grip was iron. He lifted Johan off the floor, and shook him again, so that his head jerked back and forwards, and he felt his neck might snap.

'What in the name of God are you doing, man? Put the lad down!'

The booming voice made the stoker start. He loosened his grasp on Johan, who twisted to the left and pulled away. He didn't even bother to glance at the black-clad stranger who'd saved him. Head down, he bolted back along the corridor the way he'd come, the stoker's furious yells chasing after him.

'Get back here, or I'll...'

Johan kept running.

Chapter 9

Bertha

12th & 13th April 1912

Bertha's plan to inform Captain Smith after luncheon about Mr Hoffman's terrible crime was foiled by her mother, who, as soon as they'd finished dessert, insisted that they should return to the cabin.

'You've been running wild all morning, and your hair's like rats' tails hanging out a midden. It needs a hundred strokes with a hairbrush. Then the two of us can sit and read quietly for a little while. It'll do us both good to get lost in a good book.'

Normally, Bertha would have thought the reading a splendid plan, as she was thoroughly enjoying *The Secret Garden*, but not today, not when she had an important mission to complete. She seethed with annoyance as she followed her mother back to the stuffy cabin. No wonder Sherlock Holmes managed to solve cases so quickly, when he didn't have to put up with dinner gongs and constant interference from his mother.

Reading quietly turned out to be an impossible feat. Mrs Pinsky clicked her knitting needles, and Miss

Toomey droned on and on and on about her sister Mary Ann for a solid hour, making it impossible for Bertha to concentrate on Mary Lennox's much more interesting adventures in *The Secret Garden*. Her mother had given up trying to read after five minutes and was politely pretending to care about poor Mary Ann's many misfortunes. Bertha thought her mother could have written a potted biography of every member of Ellen Toomey's extended family, if she'd been so inclined.

Boiling with frustration, Bertha put down her book and perched on the edge of the bunk, tapping her feet on the lino. When the women started fixing their hair, getting ready for afternoon tea in the Library, she rebelled. 'I'm not going. Madge isn't going to be there, so it'll be no fun at all. Marion Wright is a very nice lady, but frankly I couldn't care less if her flower girls wear peach organza or pale blue silk.'

Ellen looked scandalised.

'*Don't-Care was made to care; Don't-Care was hung.*'

'I've always found that nursery rhyme unnecessarily gruesome,' shuddered Mrs Pinsky, but Ellen wasn't finished.

'*Don't-Care was put in a pot; and boiled till he was done.*'

'I doubt he cared much about anything, after the hanging,' Bertha retorted.

Mother jabbed an enormous pin into her hat with

considerable force, turned from the mirror and gave Bertha *The Look*, but Bertha was too fed up to care.

'Let me stay in the cabin,' she pleaded. 'It'll be lovely to have some peace and quiet.'

'I dare say we'd all enjoy the peace too,' said Miss Toomey, in an acid tone, throwing open the cabin door and flouncing out.

When the women left, Bertha let out a huge sigh of relief. She wasn't used to being in the constant company of adults, and found it quite wearing. And all the adults of her acquaintance seemed to be insufferably dull, and useless role models. There wasn't an aviator, or an inventor, or a polar explorer among them.

Perhaps, once she'd spoken to Captain Smith about Mr Hoffman and he'd been arrested and thrown in the ship's dungeon (she presumed there must be one in the hold), the Captain would be so delighted that he'd make her an honorary crew member. Working on a ship might be more exciting than being a passenger.

What am I thinking? I've already got a job. I'm *The Collyer-Watt Detective Agency*'s senior partner.

She snatched up her hat, stuffing it onto her head. If she was going to find Captain Smith, she'd better do it now, as the thought of trying to explain everything to him in the presence of her mother was unappealing.

She could hear her now.

I'm so terribly sorry, Captain Smith! Bertha's always

had an over-active imagination. When she was little, she decided there were fairies living at the bottom of the garden and she wouldn't let the idea go. Our poor gardener wasn't allowed to cut back the shrubs in case a fairy was injured in the process. Come along, Bertha dear. You mustn't bother people with your silly stories.

Sighing bitterly at the unfairness of the world, Bertha picked up her autograph book and put it under her arm. She'd better have it ready, in case the Captain insisted on having evidence of the crime.

A lady was waiting for the lift to arrive, so Bertha decided to use the stairs. The less explaining she had to do, the better. Once she reached the Boat Deck, she took a deep breath, straightened her shoulders and marched up to a deckhand.

'I need to speak to Captain Smith about an important matter.'

''Fraid not. He's on the Bridge.'

The deckhand jerked his thumb in the Bridge's direction. It was the far end of the Boat Deck, eight feet up, and as inaccessible as the Moon, as getting there would mean entering both the Officers' and the 1st Class Promenade areas, both forbidden zones.

'Could you ask him to come down? It's really is terribly important.'

The deckhand didn't even attempt to disguise his grin.

'Aye, that's what I'll do, lass. I'll go and tell the Captain there are more important matters for him to attend to than steering this ship safely to New York.'

Bertha opened her mouth to protest, and then closed it again. The man was being unnecessarily sarcastic, but he *had* made an excellent point.

'Captain Smith and I have already been introduced,' she explained. 'He signed my autograph book. So if you could take me up there, I could make his acquaintance again on the Bridge? Then Captain Smith could steer the ship and I could divulge my dreadful secret.'

To Bertha's annoyance, the deckhand sniggered.

'I'm not sure he'd thank me for that, miss.'

'He will, when he realises—'

The deckhand rudely cut her off.

'Look, miss, why don't you run along and play? There's shuffleboard and quoits set up on deck for you little uns.'

Bertha gave him her fiercest scowl, but he didn't seem at all intimidated, he just strolled off, whistling Alexander's Ragtime Band.

She considered yelling at him that he couldn't whistle for toffee, but decided that would be behaviour unbecoming in a detective. It was extremely disheartening, but she'd scolded Madge for being easily discouraged, and could hardly give up at the first hurdle too.

The Captain didn't spend every moment of his time on the Bridge. She'd waylaid him out here on the first day of the voyage, when he'd been walking on deck with Mr Andrews, and asked for their autographs. He'd seemed a kindly old gent, with a white beard and twinkly eyes. When he next ventured onto the 2nd Class Promenade, she'd be waiting for him.

In the meantime, she had treasure to seek and evidence to gather.

She was about to head back to the cabin, but there was an exciting game of Kick the Can being organised on the deck by a confident, smiling lad with an American accent, who the others called Billy. Unable to resist the chance of some fun, Bertha stashed her autograph book under a lifeboat's tarpaulin and joined in the game. It was only when a bugle sounded and the boy said he needed to go to dinner, that she realised Billy was a 1st Class Passenger and it dawned her she'd just beaten William Carter, the richest boy on the ship, at Kick the Can.

That evening's meal was another dull affair, with no sign of either the Collyers or the Hoffmans and later Bertha struggled to sleep, possibly because she'd eaten far too much plum pudding. Her mind was buzzing, thoughts flying in all directions. *Would Johan be there tomorrow at ten o'clock? Would they find the treasure and if so, how would they return it to its rightful owner?*

Eventually, she stuffed her fingers in her ears to muffle Ellen Toomey's snores, and managed to fall asleep, although it was a restless sleep, haunted by a terrible dream, in which two tiny, curly-haired boys huddled on a deckchair, crying for their mother, while Bertha tried, without success, to comfort them. Then the deck beneath them vanished, evaporating like mist, leaving the deckchair bobbing on the waves, the boys screaming, and Bertha thrashing in the water.

When she woke, it was still early, and she lay for a while, listening to the steady throb of the engines, letting the nightmare recede like the tide, allowing cheerier thoughts to bubble up, until it was a reasonable hour, and she could get up and dressed.

By the time Bertha and her mother had eaten breakfast, visited the Library to change their books and returned to their cabin, it was almost ten o'clock. As Bertha buttoned her jacket, her fingers were trembling with excitement at the thought of meeting up with Johan again, and of going on a quest to find the hidden treasure. She hoped Madge would be able to join them but didn't hold out much hope, as the Collyers hadn't appeared at breakfast time.

As Bertha was about to slip from the cabin, her mother looked up from her book.

'Are you meeting up with little Marjorie Collyer this morning?'

Bertha froze. She could hardly tell her mother she was meeting up with a Swedish boy from 3rd Class.

'I expect so. Yes, probably...'

Bertha hovered in the doorway, anxious to make her escape, but her mother had other ideas.

'Take this bottle to Mrs Collyer, will you?' She handed Bertha a tiny, fairy-sized bottle with a hand-written label. 'It contains smelling salts. Tell her they might help revive her if she's feeling faint or dizzy. And ask her if she'd like an extra cover. The heating isn't working as well as it should, and we have ample blankets.'

Rosa put down her knitting.

'Charlotte Collyer's a poor soul. I can't shake the feeling this voyage was a terrible mistake for her. Planting a fruit farm in Idaho is a big undertaking for someone healthy, never mind someone so ill.'

Ellen Toomey nodded sagely. 'It'll be the death of her. Mark my words.'

Bertha's excitement fizzled out. Her words felt sticky on her tongue.

'Is Mrs Collyer going to die?'

Her mother raised her eyebrows.

'Ellen isn't a doctor, Bertha. How on earth could she answer such a question! And anyway, aren't we all going to die, at our allotted time?'

'Tuberculosis is a deadly disease, and it takes many before their time.'

Ellen was using her spooky, melodramatic voice again, and it made Bertha want to slap her. 'It took three of my young cousins. We knew they were goners when they started spitting blood.'

Bertha gulped, horrified at the thought of poor little Madge having to witness such a terrible sight, but Ellen hadn't finished doling out her opinion.

'If they'd given the 2nd Class passengers the same health checks they gave the 3rd Class, Charlotte Collyer would not have been allowed to board ship. Maybe someone should let the authorities know.'

There was a moment's chilly silence. When Bertha's mother spoke, her voice dripped ice.

'Charlotte Collyer is a lovely young woman, and her daughter is a charming companion for Bertha. We must all pray Charlotte's health improves in America and she lives a long and happy life there.'

Never before in Bertha's life had she seen her mother give *The Look* to an adult.

The lift door was closing as Bertha approached, so she broke into a run and made it just in time. Reginald, the lift boy, let her in.

'Good morning, Miss Watt. You'll be glad of your warm coat, I expect. Colder weather forecast.'

She beamed back, basking in the warmth of his smile. Reginald was by far the most handsome boy she'd ever seen, and it was a great pity that Madge was so averse to travelling in the lift, because it was Bertha's only opportunity to be in his presence.

As far as she was aware, Reginald never left his post in the lift, but somehow he appeared to be right about the weather. A brisk wind was scudding across the deck, and it definitely seemed chillier than yesterday. Bertha sauntered casually past a couple of young ladies, who were shivering in thin jackets and cotton day dresses, and walked towards the bench on which she and Johan had hopefully agreed to meet. But there was a problem. An elderly man was huddled on *their* bench, a rug on his knees, smoking a pipe. Bertha chewed on her lip, wondering what to do next, when behind her, someone whistled.

Chapter 10

Johan

Johan had been hopelessly lost on the ship for what seemed hours, scurrying along corridors and racing up and down stairways until his lungs were burning, adrenalin rushing, and every sense on hyper-alert. Panic surged in waves, and he kept glancing behind him, convinced the stoker was on his tail. Eventually, he became so disorientated that he was convinced he was retracing his steps, and began to fear the stoker might leap out in front of him, from one of the many unmarked doorways.

When, finally, Johan reached a place he recognised, the corridor leading to the 3rd Class Common Room, he almost cried with relief. Stumbling through the doorway, he rolled down the steps and landed at the feet of Nils and Oskar, who were as surprised to see him as he was glad to see them.

'What's your problem?' growled Oskar. 'Can't you behave like a normal person for once?'

'Is this a circus act you're practising?' Nils laughed

and helped to his feet. Then he looked at Johan more closely, and frowned. 'Are you alright, kid? Your neck and chin are bruised.'

Johan rubbed at his neck and examined the black streaks on his hands.

'There's some bruising, I think, but it's mostly soot,' he said, but didn't explain how either the soot or the bruises had got there.

'Well, you look like you've been in the wars. Maybe you should go and give yourself a wash. We're going to have a game of football out on deck later. Us against the Irish lads. Want to be a sub?'

Johan shook his head, grimacing at the pain the movement caused in his neck.

'I'm going to have a lie down. I feel a bit sick again.'

Ham acting, Oskar leapt backwards.

'Don't throw up over me! I'm wearing my only clean shirt!'

'Give over, Oskar.'

But Nils was grinning as he spoke, and Johan wasn't in the mood to be the butt of the joke.

Excusing himself, he limped back to the cabin, washed himself at the basin and then lay on his bunk until his heart rate slowed and the ache in his neck and shoulders started to ease. The torturous, terrifying journey back to his quarters had left him feeling shattered, but every time he closed his eyes, the soot-blackened stoker leapt in front of him, shaking him until his teeth rattled, with those furious, red-rimmed eyes fixed on his own.

Give them back, you little swine!

Little swine. Was that the same as *svinpäls* ? Had that filthy creature the cheek to call *him* a dirty beggar? At least, he thought grumpily, Pa would be pleased that his English was coming along.

To keep his mind off the stoker, Johan listed all the new words he had learned and tried to stitch them into sentences.

Sorry, little swine, please excuse me. How much does a treasure map cost?

Much later, lonely, homesick and longing for familiar accents, Johan headed back to the Common Room, and sat nursing a watery beer, while the Swedish lads sang folk songs, a Scotsman played reels on the bagpipes and the Irish danced like it was their last night on earth. Oskar became quite maudlin, and told Johan he couldn't wait until the ship reached America, because all his siblings lived in New Haven, Connecticut, and he was so looking forward to seeing them again.

'I've left most of my family in Sweden,' said Johan. He wasn't used to beer, and it was making his head feel oddly warm and fuzzy. 'My older sister Jenny lives with my father on the farm in South Dakota.' He pulled a face. 'I miss Jenny more than I do my pa.'

'Is she pretty?' Oskar grinned, taking a swig of his

beer. 'Maybe I'll visit.'

Johan growled, deep in his throat, and Oskar had the sense to shut his mouth.

Instead of retreating to the cabin when the music ended, he staggered with Nils, Oskar and the other lads to the Dining Saloon for supper, where they stuffed their faces with cabin biscuits and cheese. He even managed to slip some biscuits into his pockets for later, without being clocked by the stewards, though he ended up nibbling them in the corridor on the way back to the cabin, when the taste of stale beer and the roar of the engines made waves of sea sickness roll over him.

It was only in the middle of the night, when he lay sprawled on the bunk, unable to sleep despite his exhaustion, that his thoughts returned to the treasure map.

When the stoker had confronted him, he'd been eager to give the man the map, just so he'd let go, but hadn't been able to find it. *Where was it? Had he lost it? Or had it been taken by that girl?*

Anxiously, he patted at his pockets. Paper rustled, and a smile of relief crept across Johan's face. The map was there; he remembered now that he'd put it in his trouser pocket. The treasure was his to find, and there was nobody to stand in his way.

He fell asleep, and this time the stoker stayed out of his head. Instead, bright images of his family flickered:

his mother kneading dough, her hands white with flour, Anna darning socks at the fireside, and his brothers threshing corn, picking stones, swimming in the river, calling his name.

Johan! The water's freezing! Come and join us!

When he woke, it all came flooding back. He was alone on the Atlantic Ocean and the people he loved were far, far away. He lay on his straw mattress, eyes squeezed shut, trying to keep the image of his brothers alive, splashing in the sun-dappled river, shrieking with glee.

I'll send the tickets as soon as we land. You'll be over on the next ship. We'll all be together again.

Determination surged through him and he leapt off the bunk.

Today was the day his life was going to change for the better. With the girl's help, he was going to find the treasure.

He washed himself at the basin, raked a wet hand through his hair to smooth it down.

'You've soaked the bleedin' floor again!' grumbled Oskar, as he swung down from the bunk.

Nils and Olaf were getting dressed too, and the floor space wasn't big enough for four, but at least, Johan thought, he was up and about, and, thanks to Nils' kindness, he almost felt that he belonged.

Together, they left the cabin and used the magical,

self-flushing toilets. His worries about having to urinate over the side of the ship had been unfounded, but there was something faintly alarming about the way the water swirling in the toilet was sucked down into the depths.

'Hurry up, Johan. My stomach feels like my throat's been cut!'

The friendliness in Nils' voice warmed him, strengthening his conviction that today was going to be good. The four of them sat together, at one of the long tables. Olaf joked about being blinded by the white, and it was true that the bright lights and gleaming paint were not relaxing on the eye, but the room was spotlessly clean, and Johan felt happy to eat whatever was served, without the fears about hygiene he'd had on the ship to Hull, after seeing a gigantic rat perched on top of one of the flour barrels.

After a massive breakfast, he told Nils he was off to explore the ship, left his cabin mates to their own devices and climbed the stairs. Although, now that he'd had time to think about it, the plan to meet on the Promenade Deck had been stupid. The last thing he wanted was a repeat of yesterday's nightmarish attempts to get back to familiar territory.

But he couldn't think of a way to inform the girl of a change of plan, so decided he'd best give it a go.

There was an elderly man sitting alone on the bench, and for a moment his heart stopped. *Had the girl told her father or grandfather? Was that old man waiting to pounce as soon as he approached her?*

But then he spotted the girl, standing alone by the railing, her head turning this way and that as if she wasn't sure what to do or where to go.

He came a little nearer and whistled. She heard him, and instead of acting casual, she waved her arms like windmills, ran over and vaulted the gate like a gymnast, landing on the top step.

Johan blinked, startled. But at least they were both in his area now. It was Bertha who was on the wrong side of the gate. He pulled the map from his pocket, and held it out so she could take a good look. As she took it, he felt a shiver of excitement. It was happening. She was going to help him read the map. Once he knew where to search, he wouldn't rest until the treasure was found.

Chapter 11

Bertha

13th April 1912

Bertha pulled a face, angry with herself; that landing had been far from her best. She'd wobbled slightly, and could imagine Miss McMurray, the gymnastics teacher at Ashley Road School, rolling her eyes and critiquing her technique in her caustic-soda voice.

Bertha Watt, that landing was more reminiscent of a clumsy elephant than a graceful swan.

And now she'd landed in 3rd Class, the forbidden zone. As she took the proffered map, her heart fluttered with doubts. She glanced back over the gate and saw the elderly man on the 2nd Class Promenade pick up his copy of *The Atlantic Times* from the bench, adjusting his glasses so he could read it. He was much older, but he reminded her of her father, and sudden homesickness made her stomach churn. That old gentleman was from her middle-class world, the world of teachers, bank managers, ministers... she'd just vaulted the gate into another world, whose people lived by different standards, different rules.

I shouldn't be here. If I'm caught, I'll be in the most awful bother. Miss Toomey will tell everyone I've put all the 2nd Class passengers in danger of catching typhus or diphtheria or smallpox. My mother will write to Daddy, telling him that I'm in deep disgrace and that he must reconsider buying me a pony.

Bertha chewed her lip, glancing again at the gate, and at the old man engrossed in his newspaper. She really, really didn't want to relinquish the pony, having already decided on a feisty chestnut mare, called Primrose, or maybe Violet, or Rosabelle. Bertha had been in her mother's bad books so often recently, that she'd already decided not to give the pony a name until it was safely in their paddock.

And then she noticed Marion Wright, gliding across the deck, elegant in navy blue, a straw hat at a jaunty angle on her abundant hair. Bertha grabbed Johan's arm, and hurtled down the steps, the map clutched in her hand. When they reached the next landing, she dragged him behind a pillar, shushing his angry protests.

'Sorry for pulling you about,' she gasped. 'But I saw Marion Wright coming and thought I'd better get away before I was spotted. She's lovely but she'll tell my mother about you and then I'll have to explain everything and I can't possibly solve this case if they're interfering.'

The boy shrugged, and she remembered, yet again, that she was wasting her time trying to make conversation.

Maybe this was the worst plan in the history of plans, she thought gloomily. It's not as if she needed diamonds or gold bars—or whatever the treasure turned out to be. After all, how would she explain the acquisition of an emerald necklace or sparkly tiara to her mother?

But as Johan held out his hand to retrieve his precious map, Bertha noticed that his hands were trembling. Finding the treasure was clearly important to him. It seemed unkind to let him down. And as senior partner in *The Collyer-Watt Detective Agency*, she ought not to throw in the towel when she was so close to cracking the case, particularly not after scolding Madge for giving up too easily.

So, despite her misgivings, Bertha held on to the paper, and studied the map properly, running her finger over the words, tracing the lines and zigzags and arrows, as she tried to decipher the tiny lettering.

At the top of the crumpled page she thought she could make out the words *Well Deck*. She pointed it out to Johan.

'It looks like we need to start there. Luckily, I've come prepared.'

She'd realised as she was getting dressed that morning, that if she didn't want to get caught in a 3rd Class area, she'd need to have a disguise. Her fur-lined coat, velvet hat and new buckled shoes would have been dead giveaways, so she'd dressed in a plain blue frock and her scuffed buttoned boots. To complete the disguise, she untied a woollen scarf from around her neck, flung it over her head, and knotted it.

'I borrowed the scarf from Rosa. I didn't actually tell her I was taking it, but hopefully I'll be able to return it before she notices it's gone.'

She gave a little twirl.

'Is it a good disguise? Do I look poor enough now?'

As soon as the question spilled from Bertha's mouth, she flushed scarlet, because it seemed a terribly rude thing to have said. For once, she was glad Johan didn't speak English and was literally scratching his head, either in confusion or because he had the dreaded nits.

Mortified, she tried to distract him from her burning cheeks, by jabbing at the map with her finger and twittering like a canary.

'I think it says *Well Deck*, although it's terribly tricky to read. So I think we should start there. And I believe this shape may represent a door. I mean it could be a window, or a box, or virtually anything rectangular, but I think a door is the most likely. Let's go and find out, shall we?'

She beckoned Johan to follow and he nodded, his eyes bright and eager, full of enthusiasm for their quest, but still wary enough that he took the map back, almost ripping it. They set off, Bertha trying to ignore the doubts surging through her brain.

The Well Deck was busy with passengers enjoying the fresh air. Women clustered on the benches, their little ones on their laps or at their feet, young men perched on crates or leant against the railings. A throng of squealing children raced between the legs of the adults, engrossed in a game of tig. Bertha tugged the scarf tighter round her head, conscious of her ringlets and the ridiculous silk bows in her hair.

She closed her eyes, trying to picture the map, and in particular the location of the rectangular shape. It had been near the prow of the ship, she was sure of it. As soon as she opened her eyes she saw it, a small deckhouse with an unmarked black door, untended by a crewman, and hopefully, unlocked. She strode towards it, giving the handle a confident rattle. The door stayed shut.

It was locked. Of course it was.

Beside her, Johan clicked his teeth. His elbow jutted out, and he nudged her aside. Annoyed, she elbowed him back, harder than she'd intended. He stumbled on to the deck and grabbed the handle as he fell. Silently, the unmarked door swung open. Muttering in his odd, guttural language, Johan got to his feet, glaring at her. In response, she gestured at the open door.

'You opened it,' she whispered, torn between excitement and anxiety. If the door had been locked, it would have given her an excuse to give up this quest, slip back to the comfortable familiarity of life in 2nd

Class. *But what kind of detective would she be if she gave up when situations got scary?* Mr Holmes dealt with demonic hounds and evil criminal masterminds as a matter of course.

Bertha looked around. A steward was heading towards them. He wasn't looking directly at them, and she didn't think he'd noticed the open door. Not yet anyway.

She spoke at exactly the same time as Johan.

'Get inside, quick!' '*Komma in snabbt!*'

They stepped into a corridor; carefully, Bertha closed the door behind them.

As quietly as they could, they crept along the corridor, which was flanked at regular intervals by cabin doors. This wasn't an area for passengers, Bertha could tell. There were no bronze cherubs here, no richly patterned linoleum. This part of the ship was strictly for the crew, and she could only imagine her mother's fury if she was caught here. Luckily, the entire complement of crew seemed to be elsewhere and the only sound to be heard was the engine's roar. At the end of the corridor was a spiral staircase. Johan held up the map.

The staircase was marked as a looping squiggle. According to the rough sketch, they were still right at the front of the ship.

'The treasure's somewhere at the bottom of those stairs,' she whispered, pointing downward. Johan nodded. His eyes were round and anxious, and he kept glancing round as if he was afraid they were being followed. It wasn't helping to settle the butterflies flittering in Bertha's stomach.

Behind them, a door banged. One of the crew must have left their cabin. Bertha tugged at Johan's arm.

'We'd better get out of here,' she hissed.

The air grew warmer as they descended the steps; Bertha guessed they must be close to the boiler rooms. Her underarms were damp with sweat, and she'd have killed for a glass of cold water. As they went further, well below the waterline, the air grew chillier, and by the time they reached the bottom of the spiral staircase, it was frigid as a tomb. They were in a vast, dimly lit space, which was crammed with people's belongings: trunks, cases, crates and hatboxes, piled high and secured with netting.

'It's like Aladdin's Cave,' she whispered. Johan didn't reply, so she kept talking, to keep her nerves at bay. There was something very eerie about this place—the white netting giving everything in it the appearance of being shrouded in cobwebs.

'And somewhere, among all this stuff,' whispered Bertha, 'is the hidden treasure. We just have to find it.'

Chapter 12

Johan

13th April 1912

Johan stood at the bottom of the steps, blinking in the half-light, transfixed by the sight of the crammed hold. It made him think of the Old Norse sagas his mother told when they'd all huddled round the fire on cold winter nights, like the stories of the *Lindworm*, guarding its hoard of ancient treasure. He shivered as he remembered his mother's words.

Of course, the dragon's treasure was cursed. It brought nothing but ill to anyone foolish enough to steal it.

A scrabbling sound at his feet made him look down. To his horror, a large brown rat was scrambling over his boot.

'Oh, heavens above, it's a massive mouse!' squealed Bertha, leaping onto the second step and almost sending him flying.

Johan kicked out at the creature, but missed, and the rat scurried behind a crate, its long, naked tail slithering behind. He listened, but couldn't hear the rustling, scratching sounds he remembered from the farm. The thunder of the engines drowned out the sounds of the rats in the hold, but where there was one, there would be hundreds, he was sure. They'd need to be careful not to get bitten.

'*Jag hatar rattor*,' he muttered, and then jumped when the girl shrieked again.

'Did you say *rat*? Please tell me that wasn't a rat! I'm petrified by the very idea of rats!'

He nodded, understanding her tone, if not the words. It seemed they had one thing in common at least.

Bertha tightened the scarf around her head and gave a deep, heartfelt sigh.

'Well, we'd better get on with this mission, so we can get out of here in double quick time.'

She leapt down the steps, and although he had no idea what she'd just said, he was impressed by her courage, as he was afraid to move, in case another rat scurried across his path. When she held out her hand, he guessed she wanted to look at the map, but he was reluctant to let it go.

'*Kom och se*.'

She got the gist, and looked over his shoulder while he unfolded the paper. Johan stared down at it, trying to will the foreign words into sense, wishing he didn't need help from anyone.

He guessed that the arrows on the map had been drawn when the baggage holds were empty. Now that it had been filled, it was impossible to take the route suggested on the map, as it would have meant clambering over the top of a massive crate. The girl spoke again, enunciating every syllable. It didn't make her alien language any easier to understand.

'We can go round this big crate. I wonder what's in it and to whom it belongs, don't you? If we squeeze past those trunks, it should be doable, though we might have to do a bit of climbing. It'll be easy for me. I've climbed a Munro, right to the top. Munros are Scottish mountains. Do you have mountains in Sweden?'

He shrugged, hoping a shrug was an appropriate response, and pulled the map away from the girl's tugging fingers, stuffing it back in his pocket.

When they squeezed past the crate, Johan peered through the gap between the wooden slats, and stopped dead. There was treasure inside—a motor car—a beautiful Renault limousine. His fingers reached in and a smile flickered on his lips as he touched the car's glossy burgundy bodywork, its gleaming brass fittings.

One day, I will own a car like that. Pa always says cars are for half-wits, and will never replace the horse, but he's stuck in the past. I'll take my mother for drives in my new car, and John and Leo and Rheinhold and Gosta can sit in the back. Pa can stay on the farm and muck out the horses. Who'll be the half-wit then?

Bertha prodded him in the back.

'Can we get a move on, please? My mother will be mustering a search party if I'm late for luncheon.'

He dragged himself away from the car, and walked on. At the other side of the limousine were more tidy piles of baggage, all secured by ropes and covered in netting. It all looked very organised and efficient, but Johan spotted another rat squirming out of a crate, a scrap of material dangling from its jaws, and was glad his own possessions were safely in the cabin.

Bertha was speaking, her voice extra loud. She seemed to imagine that raising her voice made it more intelligible, and he didn't have the words to tell her she was hurting her throat for no benefit. But she obviously wanted to look at the map, because when he pulled it from his pocket, she snatched it out of his hand.

'I'm not sure what this square represents.' Bertha pushed the map under his nose. 'What do you think it's meant to be?'

She gestured at the shape as she spoke. He nodded, looked around. There was nothing obviously square. Then he looked up, and saw it. A hatch in the roof, designed for lowering bulky items down from the deck above. As he pointed it out to Bertha, he felt a shiver of excitement course down his spine. They were within feet of the treasure. Bertha grinned at him.

'Race you!'

Boots clattering, they ran down the narrow alley

between the crates. Johan almost crashed into Bertha when she stopped dead beneath the hatch.

'The safe should be in this area,' she said, waving her arms in a circular motion. 'Perhaps it's behind one of these pillars?'

He looked to where she was gesturing. It made sense. He started checking each pillar, and behind the second one, about four feet from the ground, he found it. The box had been painted white to blend in with the pillar, and if he hadn't been looking, he'd never have noticed it, as it was much thinner and smaller than he'd expected. It was a metal box, roughly made, with a hinged door. A small padlock held it shut.

'*Skatten*,' he whispered to Bertha. She turned, a guilty look on her face, and a vast, ostrich-plumed hat on her head.

He pointed at the box.

'*Skatten*.'

Bertha threw the hat back in its cylindrical box, banging down the lid.

'Oh, we've found the treasure!' she gasped, clambering over a trunk to reach him. Her cheeks were scarlet, but she seemed to have plenty of energy left; the girl bounded like a mountain goat.

She stood on her tiptoes, examining the metal box.

'It isn't very big, is it? Not big enough for gold bars or a diamond tiara. Perhaps an emerald bracelet, or a purse, stuffed with banknotes?'

He shrugged, having no idea what she was saying.

Bertha turned, her face glowing with excitement. 'George's letter mentioned a key. Johan, do you have the key? If not, I'm sure we could prise the box open, or pick the lock, or...'

He shrugged again, drew the key from his jacket pocket and, with shaking fingers, inserted it in the lock. His head was bursting with wild imaginings. He'd buy his mother and siblings tickets for the *Titanic*'s next voyage. They'd be so thrilled, particularly his mother, who must be so tired of managing alone. He could picture her, reclining in a deckchair on the Promenade Deck, sipping tea from a china cup, cosy in a fur stole. Then his dreams mixed with his memories and he had to squeeze his eyes shut to stop the tears, as he remembered his last sight of her. She'd been standing at the door, fear and exhaustion etching lines on her forehead. But she'd smiled at him, love shining in her bright blue eyes.

'Take care of yourself, son,' she'd said, pulling him close. And he'd hugged her briefly and walked away without looking back, drowning in worries about his journey, his future. His mother had been abandoned, left to scratch a living on the old homestead, left to care for his brothers, with only Anna to help. If only he'd turned around for a last glimpse of her, because that awful, heart-wrenching conviction that he'd never see her again, wouldn't leave him.

Bertha poked him in the ribs and he jumped.

'Is the lock stiff?' she asked, 'Do you want me to try?'

Her excited voice brought him back to the present. This treasure would change everything.

He turned the key, and the hinge on the padlock dropped. As Bertha removed it from the lock, Johan noticed that her fingers were trembling too, and she was bouncing on her toes, fizzing with excitement, eager to see what was inside. He was all too aware, that for this girl, it was just a game. For him, it could make all the difference in the world.

The door swung open. Hardly aware that he was holding his breath, Johan peered inside, Bertha on her tiptoes at his side.

'What's inside? What can you see? Let me look!'

He'd been expecting to see the gleam of gold, or the glitter of diamonds, not the dull glint of a tobacco tin and the creamy pallor of a clay pipe. He pulled the items out, along with a photograph, tucked under the tin. Then he felt inside, the rough metal base snagging on his fingertips. The box was empty. There was no treasure.

Bertha snatched the tin from him, and scanned the label.

'*Gallaghers Two Flakes Tobacco*. Let's hope the treasure's in here!'

But as she prised the tin open, the rich aroma of

tobacco spilled out. It reminded him of his father, and that his future now lay with him, working his fingers to the bone on the farm in Clay County, his loved ones thousands of miles away.

Bertha plonked herself down on a crate.

'Not my idea of treasure,' she sighed. He got the gist, but compared to his, her disappointment was as shallow as a puddle.

Defeated, Johan slumped beside her, and gazed at the photograph in his hands. A square-jawed young man in an ill-fitting suit, stood next to a thin woman in a striped frock with a lace collar. They wore serious expressions, but you could sense their pride. All their focus was on the child who sat in front of them, a plump little queen on a wicker throne, resplendent in a frothy white dress, a huge bow tied in her fair curls, and her fat little fists clutching a wooden rattle.

Bertha took the photo, turning it over. There was writing on the back, in the same loopy, untidy hand as the letter.

'*Me, Emily and Alice, December 1910,*' she read aloud. Her hand flew to her mouth. She turned the photo back over and pointed at the child. 'Alice! His little girl. His treasure. She's dead. Remember? It said in the letter that she died of typhus fever. No wonder Francis wants the photo back.'

Treasure... Skatten Dead... dod. There was no treasure.

His dreams were dead.

Anger surged through him. He felt that he'd been taken on a wild goose chase, that Bertha had raised his hopes—only to dash them. He threw the tobacco tin, and it smacked against a trunk, its contents scattering. Then he dropped the clay pipe, and stamped on it, again and again, his boot raising a cloud of white dust.

Bertha was still clutching the photograph and he snatched it from her hand, intending to rip it.

She screamed as though he'd slapped her.

'*No! You mustn't! It's his treasure!*'

Johan flopped back down on the crate, letting his hand drop, and the photograph floated to the ground, the sepia figures spinning, as though they were on a carousel.

It landed on the floor, and the woman in the picture stared at him, her eyes filled with accusation.

In despair, he put his head in his hands.

He'd failed. The treasure had been his only hope.

And now it was lost.

Chapter 13

Bertha

13th April 1912

Bertha had watched, frozen in horror, as Johan smashed the clay pipe to smithereens, but when she thought he was going to destroy poor little Alice's photograph, a flame of anger sparked inside her.

She leapt up, grabbed the photo from the ground, and turned on Johan, hands on her hips.

'Why would you do something so horrible?' she yelled. 'Don't you see how precious that photograph must be to poor Francis? He has lost his little girl, and the photo is all he has left...'

Her voice tailed away as Johan looked up and she realised he was crying. For a moment, she stood, floundering, utterly out of her depth. In the rule book she followed, girls were allowed to cry. Boys weren't. It seemed the rules were changing at a rate of knots, and she wasn't sure how to cope.

Gulping down her discomfort, she put the photo in the pocket of her dress, and sat back down beside Johan giving his hand an awkward pat.

'I'm sorry. I know you're sad that it wasn't real treasure. I'd been hoping for a gold tiara myself. But it doesn't really matter, does it? It's not the end of the world.'

But it seemed that it was. All the brightness had left the boy's eyes. He looked utterly desolate and she had no idea how to comfort him. Whenever she got upset at home in Aberdeen, her father would try to distract her with a joke or a magic trick involving a handkerchief, but she was skilled in neither comedy nor magic. Maybe she should copy her mother's strategy instead, and advise Johan to give his face a good wash and blow his nose. The trouble was, she had a feeling that Johan's distress was about something more major than failing an arithmetic test or not getting top prize in gymnastics.

She put her hand on his shoulder, attempting another pat.

'Lämna *mig ifred!'   Leave me alone!

Johan pulled away and leapt to his feet. Bertha realised he was about to run for it, and grabbed at his arm, horrified by the prospect of being abandoned in this dark, rat-infested place.

But he shook her off and started to run down one of the narrow alleys, heading back towards the spiral staircase. Bertha's thoughts whirled in panicky spirals. *What if he locked her in?* If she was trapped down here until the end of the voyage, her mother would search everywhere in 2nd Class, but then she'd have to presume

Bertha had fallen overboard. Nobody would think to look for her in the hold.

Johan was nearly at the staircase. She scrambled after him, kicking out at the trailing netting which tangled round her feet. Trying to find a short cut, she threw herself over a pile of cases, and sent one crashing to the ground.

'Wait for me, Johan!' she yelled. 'What are you mad at me for? You're being really mean!'

He must have heard the panic in her voice, because he stopped, and turned back, even extending a hand to help her over the teetering pile of crates. But he was muttering angrily under his breath, as if all of this was her fault, as though she'd tricked him.

The metal treads rattled as he stomped up the stairs, breathing like a dragon, and as she followed him up, anger rose in her own chest, bubbling in the heat of the boiler rooms. Johan reached the top, and clattered along the corridor as if he was being chased by the hounds of hell. When he burst through the door to the Well Deck and let it slam back in her face, it was the last straw.

She marched out on to the deck and raced after him, yelling his name. Johan stopped dead. He turned round, rubbed at his red-rimmed eyes as if trying to erase the sight of her. Bertha marched up to him, hands on her hips.

'How dare you!' she stormed. 'All I did was try and

help you, and you're being insufferably rude!'

A group of children stopped their game of ring toss, and stared, open mouthed. Some youths started to point and snigger. Bertha narrowed her eyes at them, then turned on Johan, and growled the worst insult imaginable.

'Well, all I can say is that you are no gentleman.'

Fizzing with annoyance, she stormed off, without a second glance. As she approached the steward at the gate, she tugged the scarf from her hair, holding it up for his inspection.

'My best scarf blew on to the Well Deck. I had to go and rescue it. My Daddy gave it to me for Christmas.' She lied blithely, not caring if he believed her or not. The steward held open the gate, a cheeky grin on his face.

'Was that young lad helping you look for your scarf?' he said, tone gently mocking. 'You'd think he'd have told you it was there all the time, wrapped round your head like a pirate's bandana.'

She flounced past the steward, head held high. When she reached the first bench, she rolled the scarf into a ball and tucked it behind the bench's slatted back, afraid Mrs Pinsky would spot it. Then she plonked herself down, breathing hard. She'd thought it would be fun to tear up the rule book, but she had to admit that she was finding life without it rather more discombobulating than she'd imagined.

Already this morning, she'd stolen a scarf, trespassed in the hold, and broken so many of her mother's rules that she'd be a hundred before the promised pony materialised. And she thought guiltily, what was sauce for the goose, was sauce for the gander. What she'd said to Johan had been stupid. He'd as much right as she did to make his own rules.

Slamming doors in people's faces was rude, there was no doubt in her mind about that, but Johan didn't *have* to behave like any of the gentlemen of her acquaintance; holding doors open, standing up when a woman entered a room, any more than she had to act like a young lady. He was heading for a new life across the sea too. She wished she'd been able to ask where he was going, and why.

Bertha pulled the photograph of Francis and his family from her coat pocket and was gazing at it when the luncheon gong sounded. She looked at her gloves, and saw that they were smeared with filth from the hold. Dusty cobweb threads trailed from her coat.

She could already picture the look on her mother's face.

Luckily for Bertha, Mrs Watt was so engaged in conversation with Marion Wright and Kate Buss that she scarcely noticed the state of her daughter's clothes, and Bertha was able to tuck into three lamb chops and two helpings of custard pudding without anybody seeing fit to comment. Frustratingly, as Bertha was desperate to relate the whole story, Madge didn't appear, so when she'd finished eating, Bertha went and knocked on the door of the Collyer's cabin.

Harvey Collyer answered. Bertha could see his wife, propped up on pillows, an old-fashioned Paisley shawl draped over her shoulders. Madge perched beside her on a stool, sewing a sampler. Bertha smiled politely, lips firmly closed.

'Good afternoon, Mr Collyer. I was wondering if you could spare Marjorie for half an hour?' A delighted grin lit Madge's face, but she hid it behind the sampler's hoop. Mr Collyer turned to his wife.

'Would that be alright, Charlotte? The child could do with some fresh air.'

'Yes, of course. It's lovely to see you again, Bertha. I'm so sorry that I'm not up and dressed, but for some reason, I'm terribly tired today. Hopefully, tomorrow will be better and I'll be able to take tea with your mother and the other ladies.'

There was a slight tremor in Charlotte's voice. Her dark hair trailed over thin, hunched shoulders, and her face was as white as her nightgown. Bertha was horribly reminded of Tennyson's *The Lady of Shallot*; her pale, pale corpse floating down the stream. *Was Ellen Toomey right? Was Charlotte Collyer going to die?*

Bertha wrapped a protective arm round Madge's

shoulder and hugged her close as they walked towards the Library.

'I've got such a lot to tell you!' she whispered. 'You'll never believe what happened. I went looking for the treasure!'

They found a quiet spot, in a far corner. Madge listened wide-eyed, hugging her doll, as Bertha told her about *The Case of the Strange Boy and The Treasure Map*, from its exciting beginning to its anticlimactic end. Happily, Madge was very taken with the middle of the story.

'Oh, my goodness, Bertha!' she gasped. 'Weren't you terrified out of your wits, down there in that terrible, gloomy place?'

Bertha paused, and considered the question. She *had* been afraid, briefly, when she'd thought Johan was going to lock her in the hold, but for most of the time she'd been too involved in trying to solve the case to be scared. In fact, now that she had time to think about it, she'd actually been terribly brave.

She turned to her autograph book, lying open on one of the writing desks and began to scribble her case notes.

Case 2: The Strange Boy and the Treasure Map

Conclusion

It turns out that Francis's 'treasure' was not quite as expected. It was neither a pirate's chest, nor a burglar's hoard, but something much more precious: a photograph of a little girl by the name of Alice, unfortunately deceased. The detectives of The Collyer-Watt Agency solemnly vow to return the photograph to its original owner.

Berth turned and smiled at Madge, who was reading over her shoulder.

'Fortunately, I have an excellent memory, an essential quality in a good detective, and have committed the sender's address to memory. Francis lives at 72, Templemore Street, Bally... something in Belfast. So we can post the photograph to him. We can purchase postage stamps from the Purser's Office.'

'Oh, poor Francis will be so happy to have the photograph of his little girl back, Bertha! I think that's a very satisfactory ending, all things considered.'

Bertha gave a cautious nod, glad that Madge agreed, but unable to dispel the feeling that this had not been a completely successful case for *The Collyer-Watt Detective Agency*.

'I wish I knew why Johan got so upset,' she murmured. 'You'd think he'd have been glad it all turned out so satisfactorily. I guess his heart must have been set on finding gold.'

She stopped talking, remembering the anger in

Johan's eyes, his terrible distress when he'd discovered that Francis's treasure was worthless. The boy wasn't wealthy; that was evident by his clothes, by his 3rd Class ticket. Perhaps he'd wanted the treasure for something important. Maybe she should have been more sympathetic. Would it be a good idea to try and get in touch with him again? Perhaps he needed another project, to distract him from his unhappiness. "*Busy hands are happy hands*" was one of her mother's favourite sayings.

'Perhaps Johan might be interested in helping us solve *The Mystery of Mr Hoffman*?' she said thoughtfully.

'I've no idea, Bertha. Don't you need to speak English to be a good detective?'

Bertha sighed, deciding Madge might be right. After all, even if he had the necessary language skills, what could Johan do, when he was in 3rd Class and Mr Hoffman and the boys were in 2nd?

She and Madge would have to solve their next case alone. It was just a matter of coming up with a plan.

Chapter 14

Johan

Johan's anger crashed like stormy waves battering against rocks. Fingers flying, he ripped the stupid, useless map into a hundred tiny pieces and tossed them over the railings. When he leaned over, wanting the bitter satisfaction of watching his lost hopes drown, the pieces had vanished, spirited away by the wind. When he turned away from the railings, he realised he'd been spotted. Two tiny boys in crumpled, linen sailor suits, were watching him from above, wide-eyed, their small fists gripping the gate which separated them from the 3rd Class area.

The elder was dark-haired, but the younger boy's fair curls reminded Johan of his youngest brother, Gosta. There was something so appealing about both boys, that despite his distress, Johan found his face creasing in a smile. The younger boy stuck his thumb in his mouth, hiding shyly behind his brother. The older one squashed his face against the gate and called out to Johan.

'*As-tu vu Mama? Elle est perdue.*'

Johan understood one word... *Mama*. They were looking for their mother. He glanced behind the boys, to see if she might be about, but could only see two elderly ladies in steamer chairs, and a dark-haired man who was charging past the women, heading for the gate. There was a scowl on his face, and the tails of his frockcoat flapped behind him. To Johan's alarm, as the man reached the gate, he brandished his fist, and bawled in an unfamiliar tongue. '*Comment osez-vous! Éloignez-vous de mes enfants!*'

How dare you! Get away from my children!

He spat the words, and snatched both boys into his arms, as if they'd been in danger.

Johan might not have been able to understand what the man was saying, but he caught the rage, and the fear, in his voice, and was taken aback by it.

'*Jag gjorde inget fel!*' he insisted, putting up his hands, as though the man was a policeman, come to arrest him. *I did nothing wrong!*

The younger boy wriggled in his father's arms.

'*Où est Mama?*' he wailed, tears spurting like geysers.

The man's eyes blazed with a rage so intense that Johan stilled, hands in the air, frozen like a troll at sunrise. He seemed to think his son's distress was all Johan's fault.

As the man stomped off, the older boy lifted his head from his father's shoulder and held out both of his pudgy little hands towards Johan.

'*Où est Maman?*'

They disappeared into the deckhouse, but for a long moment, Johan stood on the steps leading up to the gate, rooted to the spot, caught by the notion that the little boy had been pleading for help in finding his mother.

But what could he do, from the wrong side of the gate? These children belonged in a world he wasn't allowed to enter.

'Oh no! Look, Nils, it's the Puke Monster. Watch he doesn't throw up all over your boots!'

Oskar's mocking tones dragged Johan back to earth. Maybe he was projecting his own misery onto a perfectly normal family scene. The mother of those little boys was probably sipping tea right now, in a deckchair on the 2nd Class Promenade Deck, enjoying five minutes' peace. But he couldn't shake the feeling that they'd needed help, and he should have done more.

Nils grinned at him, and slapped him on the back.

'Are you coming for food, or aren't you? I've asked you three times already!'

Johan managed a watery smile.

'Food sounds good,' he said. 'I'm ravenous.'

As he followed Nils and Oskar to the Dining Room, it dawned on him that all his anger had fizzled out, like a damp flare. It had happened when he'd noticed those two small boys at the gate. Their sweet faces had made even him forget his unhappiness for a moment. But now, he was unable to shake the feeling that he'd let those children down. Somehow, he vowed, he'd try and find them again, to check that all was well.

Unfortunately, whether it was the roast mutton, the boiled potatoes, the creamy rice pudding, or a surfeit of all three, as he finished his meal Johan's seasickness returned with a vengeance.

Nils squinted at him.

'You okay, mate? You're looking a bit green.'

'The Puke Monster Strikes Again!' sniggered Oskar, as Johan staggered to his feet, clutching his stomach, attacked by terrible cramps. The all too familiar waves of nausea began rising in his throat, as he ran off, anxious not to be sick in front of everyone.

'Head for the toilets, not our cabin!' roared Oskar. 'I'm sick of it stinking of vomit!'

Johan did as he was told, and veered towards the toilets, retching as he raced down the corridor. The rest of that miserable Saturday was spent with his head down a self-flushing toilet, in a cramped cubicle which reeked of new paint and disinfectant. Eventually, he decided enough was enough, and crawled back to his bunk, whey-faced and dizzy, where he fell into an exhausted sleep. At first, when he woke, disorientated, in an empty cabin, he had no idea whether it was day or night, until he saw a leather Bible lying on Nils' bunk and guessed it must be Sunday morning, or even later.

He got up, and stood at the sink, swaying slightly. His face in the small mirror was ghost- white, his hair sticky with sweat. He was still fully dressed, but his boots lay on the floor, covered in a film of grey dust from the hold.

There had been no treasure, he remembered, and he'd been devastated. But strangely, it was the memory of those two small faces pressed against the gate, those sweet little boys, looking for their Mama, that haunted him now. He couldn't get those outstretched arms, those huge, round eyes out of his head.

Groaning, he turned on the tap, and stuck his head under the gushing cold water. He straightened up, shaking his wet hair so that a spray of water arced across the cabin, splattering the walls. Then he faced his reflection in the mirror.

Somehow, he needed to keep his own family together, bring them all to America. His little brothers needed him to be strong, to fight for them. If there was no treasure, then he'd have swallow his disappointment, and shoulder his responsibilities. Somehow, he'd have to earn his own money, and squirrel it away until he'd gathered enough for their tickets. If he knew his father, he'd be in no great rush to bring over the two youngest. Being so little, they were more hindrance than help on the farm. Pa would see them simply as two extra mouths to feed, and he'd be happy to leave them over in Sweden with their mother until they were old enough to be of proper use to him. Johan straightened his tie. It was going to be up to him, and him alone. He fingered the coins in the lining of his jacket, and then rummaged in his pockets.

They were empty. *The map was gone.* He bit his lip as the memories flooded back, making him squirm. He'd shredded the map, smashed the clay pipe, and strewn tobacco across the floor of the hold. Heat rose up his neck as he remembered how he'd taken his fury out on the girl, who'd only been trying to help. He opened the door of the cabin, striding along the corridor, filled with new energy and purpose. He'd head to the 2nd Class Promenade Deck, find the girl and muster enough English words for an apology. He'd find those little boys too, prove to himself that everything was fine, and it was all a misunderstanding. Perhaps he could start doing some odd jobs for the stewards to earn himself a few coins.

But when he walked outside, into a bitter wind, and headed up the steps towards the 2nd Class Promenade Deck, the scene could not have been more different from the previous day. The decks were deserted, save for two crew members, distant figures, straightening the davits on one of the lifeboats. Perhaps it was the change in the weather that kept people inside: the choppy grey sea and the threatening clouds? But it dawned on Johan for the first time, that there were no lifeboats at all on the 3rd Class deck areas, and that now he came to think about it, there seemed far more passengers aboard this ship than the existing lifeboats could possibly accommodate.

Then, to his surprise, he saw two figures, walking past the deckhands. As they drew nearer, he recognised the girl, by her long stride, and tangled curls. Her arm was draped round the shoulder of a smaller girl, her little sister perhaps. If Bertha had been alone, he'd have called to her from the gate.

Please, excuse me. Sorry.

But she wasn't alone, so Johan said nothing. He slipped away, heading back inside; he would try again tomorrow. He had no idea, then, that for this ship, tomorrow wouldn't come.

Chapter 15

Bertha

Sunday 14th April 1912

When Bertha woke early on Sunday morning to the sound of Ellen Toomey's pig-like snores, she decided that despite all the excitement of being aboard the biggest ship in the world, she'd be rather glad when this voyage was over.

The thought of the little attic bedroom in Oregon, which her father had described so vividly in his letters, was becoming more appealing by the minute. She squeezed her eyes shut, picturing the white painted bedstead, polished floorboards and rose-patterned wallpaper. There was a window seat, with gingham cushions, overlooking the garden. It would be lovely to wake to the sound of birdsong instead of the low, rumbling thunder of *Titanic's* engines—although she'd miss Madge and the little Hoffman boys.

Bertha's eyes snapped open.

The Collyer-Watt Detective Agency had only a few days left. She and Madge had a lot to do before this ship reached New York. *The Mystery of Mr Hoffman* was no nearer to being solved, despite their best efforts. In fact, Mr Hoffman had refused point blank yesterday afternoon to let them take Lolo and Momon for a walk. When Lolo had begged to be allowed, he had grown quite agitated, and had marched the boys back to his cabin. It was downright strange behaviour. Even her mother thought Mr Hoffman was "*rather over possessive of his children*" and "*oddly abrupt*". Bertha had overheard her say as much to Marion Wright at dinner last night and she had felt quite triumphant.

She'd been right all along. There *was* something strange going on. But *The Mystery of Mr Hoffman* was proving to be a very tricky case to crack.

A brilliant idea occurred to her and Bertha leapt off the top bunk, whooping like Geronimo, and landed on top of Miss Toomey's carpet bag. Sadly, Miss Toomey was awake and noticed.

'What on earth are you doing, you silly girl!' she roared, sitting up on her couch bed. 'If you've broken anything I'll-'

Bertha stared at Miss Toomey, thinking she looked very peculiar with her hair down. Stiff, lacquered tendrils stuck out in all directions, like writhing snakes. Her lime green, beribboned nightgown added to the monstrous effect. She was about to point out Ellen's astonishing resemblance to Medusa, when her mother gave a warning cough.

'Bertha dear, why did you get out of bed in such a hurry? If you're going to the bathroom, put your coat on over your nightdress, and don't forget your slippers.'

Bertha clamped her mouth shut and fetched her coat and slippers; she wasn't about to explain her idea to her mother; it was doubtful she'd approve. Madge was sure to go along with the plan, which was to take Mr Hoffman's fingerprints and post them to Scotland Yard, with an accompanying letter outlining the suspicions of *The Collyer-Watt Detective Agency*. Bertha had developed a gut feeling that a suitable opportunity to explain everything to the Captain was not going to arise, so going direct to the police seemed like an excellent alternative. And fingerprints were crucial in capturing criminals, she was sure of it, although she was less sure about the logistics.

As Bertha trotted along the corridor towards the toilets, she wondered how she and Madge could manage to obtain Mr Hoffman's prints without being noticed. But when a lady passed her, clutching a leather-bound Bible to her bosom, Bertha remembered, with a sinking heart, that today was a Sunday. In Aberdeen—and knowing her luck, the entire world—, Sunday was treated as a day of rest, and was therefore the dullest day in the week. There was no chance of anything exciting happening on a Sunday, Bertha thought glumly. No chance at all. Growling with annoyance, Bertha swung the toilet door so hard she almost clobbered a poor woman in the face.

As Sunday plodded by, Bertha's gloomy prediction seemed to be coming true.

After breakfast, there was a church service, mercifully short, and then to Bertha's immense frustration, her mother insisted that she spend the afternoon in *"quiet, reflective pursuits."*

'By those I mean reading your Bible, sewing, or writing a letter to Daddy. These are pastimes not punishments, so you can take that look off your face right now. You and Marjorie have spent most of this voyage running riot round the ship, and you can do it all again tomorrow; just not on a Sunday.'

The trouble was that Bible reading, sewing, and letter writing ruled out any prospect of surreptitious fingerprint taking, particularly as she was confined to the Library with her mother and the other ladies, and Mr Hoffman was very unlikely to come and spend time in their company. The ladies asked too many awkward questions about Mr Hoffman's poor dead wife.

Kicking her heels against the chair, Bertha sat at one of the desks and wrote a long letter to her father, telling him all about the daring deeds of *The Collyer-Watt Detective Agency* and suggesting that he might like to submit an article about them to *The Oregonian*. Thinking of Madge led to her next suggestion: that her father might want to establish a fruit farm on his own patch of land, which could be managed by the Collyers. It seemed to Bertha to be a perfectly workable plan. After all, surely fruit would grow as well in Oregon as in Idaho, and how could she be expected, she wrote passionately, to bear the pain of saying goodbye to her newest and dearest friend?

After Bertha had posted the letter to her father at the Purser's Office, having been assured that it would arrive at the house in Oregon before she did, she considered writing the promised letter to Francis too, but then changed her mind, oddly reluctant to let go of the photograph stuffed in her coat pocket.

In the late afternoon, she and Madge went for a walk on the Promenade Deck but it wasn't a successful expedition, as the weather had turned bitterly cold, and Madge was miserable, stuffing her hands into her coat pocket, and complaining they were frostbitten.

'You'll never make a polar explorer if you can't cope with a little chill in the air,' Bertha snorted, but if forced under torture, she'd have had to admit she'd just crossed polar explorer off her own list of possible career paths. As they headed back to the deckhouse, she glanced behind her, and was sure she saw Johan at the gate, but before she could say a word, he'd vanished like a ghost.

Dinner was a splendid affair, but just as Bertha began to think Sundays aboard ship weren't so bad after all, somebody announced that there was to be an evening service. To her intense dismay, Mother insisted that she should accompany her to that too.

'Can't I read Bible verses in the cabin? Or say double-length prayers at bedtime? I can't sit through two sermons in one day! It'll be so boring!' Miss Toomey's eyebrows lifted, two black furry moths, about to fly off her face.

Behind Ellen's back, Bertha's mother winked.

'It's a hymn service, Bertha. There will be no sermon, just singing. You'll enjoy it.'

The hymn service was held in the 2nd Class Dining Saloon and was presided over by Reverend Carter. Much to Bertha's delight, Madge was there with her parents, but sadly Mr Hoffman wasn't. It was disappointing, as Bertha had decided to "*borrow*" his hymn sheet and post it to Scotland Yard for fingerprinting. When she wondered aloud why the Hoffmans were absent, Bertha's mother said she expected they were Jewish, and anyway, the boys were much too young to be kept up so late.

Nice Mr Norman played the piano. He was a charming young man from Edinburgh, and Bertha's mother had taken a great liking to him. While Marion Wright was singing *There is a Green Hill*, Bertha heard Mother whispering to Kate that it was rather a pity Marion was already betrothed, because she and Mr Norman made such a handsome couple.

Bertha enjoyed the service, as singing was one of her favourite things. However during the hymn *Eternal*

Father, Strong to Save, when the congregation sang the words *"Oh, hear us when we cry to Thee, For those in peril on the sea"* she felt a shiver run down her spine. Later, it seemed to Bertha that they'd all tempted fate that evening.

At ten o'clock the service ended. A steward had laid out coffee and slices of cake and Reverend Carter made a short speech.

'We are all looking forward to our imminent arrival in New York. It is the first time that there have been hymns sung on this boat on a Sunday evening, but we trust and pray it won't be the last.'

'Amen to that,' said Bertha's mother. 'Let us hope these are the first cheerful Sunday services of many aboard the *Titanic.* Although I have to say, I'm looking forward to spending next Sunday in a real church, listening to the chime of bells instead of the roar of a ship's engine.' She turned to Bertha, who wasn't even trying to stifle her yawns. 'Time for bed, dear, It's very late.'

For once Bertha was glad to go. It had been a long day, and in the main, insufferably dull, as Sundays always were. She might have known that the usual routines would be adhered to, even aboard ship, and had to live in hope that Sundays would be more fun in America.

After prayers and a cursory wash at the sink, Bertha pulled on her nightdress, and climbed into her bunk. Overall, she decided, the voyage aboard the *Titanic* had been quite a thrill, but the prospect of arriving in New York in a couple of days was even more exciting. Her mother was planning to visit relatives in Boston, she'd see her father again for the first time in months, they'd travel to Oregon and soon, very soon, she could begin her amazing new life as an *All-American* girl.

The only downside was she'd be saying goodbye to Madge. Unless Bertha's father took her up on her brilliant suggestion of starting a fruit farm, it wasn't likely the two girls would meet again, not in a country the size of America. They really must, she decided, make the most of their last couple of days aboard ship. After all, she and Madge still had a case to solve. *The Case of Mr Hoffman* was getting more mysterious by the moment and she hadn't yet had the opportunity to discuss it with the Captain. Yawning, she pulled her blanket over her head, let her eyelids close, and drifted off to sleep.

In her dream, she was bobbing on Loch Ness, aboard a wooden rowing boat. Her father was at the helm, joking with her mother, who was wearing a broad-brimmed hat, to keep the sun off her face. It felt more like a lovely memory than a dream, until the day began to turn cold, and a freezing wind started to scud across the loch.

'We need to get to shore!' called her father. 'Start rowing, for God's sake!'

Terror gripped Bertha's throat. She pointed a shaking finger.

'Look, Daddy, the water's turning to ice!'

As she watched in horror, a film of ice formed on the surface of the water. The little boat cut through the ice, with eerie cracking sounds which made Bertha shiver. They began to drift past icebergs, high as Ben Nevis. Bertha reached out to touch one. It was smooth as glass; so cold it burned her hand. And then she heard a terrible grinding, grating sound. Underwater, jagged ice was scraping along the tiny boat's hull, splitting it apart. Ice-cold water swirled round Bertha's ankles, and she opened her mouth to scream.

Chapter 16

Johan

14th April 1912

Nils' head bobbed around the cabin door.

'How are you doing?'

His bright smile faded when he saw Johan lying on his bunk.

'You need to stop moping around, kid! It's time to get up and at 'em.'

He pulled Johan to his feet, shoved his jacket into his arms. Johan complied meekly, and didn't mention that he hadn't been moping, he'd been working for several hours in the crew's galley, filleting mackerel. The cook had only coughed up a few pennies, but the coins now jingling in his pocket were going to add up—he was determined of that—and equally determined that the money should remain his secret.

Nils pulled a comb from his pocket, and tidied his hair, then attempted to tug it through Johan's. He gave up and rammed Johan's cap on his head.

'There, you look almost respectable. You're not sick any more, are you? Come out with us tonight. You might even have a good time. There's going to be ragtime music from the Yanks, dancing and maybe even some decent company, if Oskar can talk those Irish lasses into coming along.'

Johan followed Nils out of the cabin; doing as he was told seemed easier than arguing.

The Common Room was mobbed, the music loud, and as Nils had predicted, the evening was more fun than Johan had imagined. He'd slept so late that day that he wasn't tired and it was such a relief that his stomach had settled, and he could watch the dancers whirl around to the music, without having to rush out of the room to throw up. At supper time they all charged along to the Dining Hall, and soaked up the beer with bread and pastries.

The beer was flowing and many of the men were getting steadily more inebriated. Johan stuck to water, and by eleven, he was still in the Common Room, sitting in a corner with Nils, chatting about their lives in Sweden and their plans for the future.

'I'm the eldest of six, and my parents want me to study agriculture for a year and then come back to Sweden,' said Nils, taking a swig of beer. 'I'm going to see how it goes. If I meet a nice American girl, I might want to stay a lot longer!'

He jerked his head in Oskar's direction.

'What's that dope up to now? He'll get himself thrown

overboard if he's not careful.'

Oskar had staggered up to an enormous Irishman and now stood in front of him, elbow raised, challenging the man to an arm-wrestling competition. Nils put his beer glass down, wiped foam from his moustache and stood up, sighing heavily.

'Why does Oskar always have to do stupid stuff when he gets drunk? That big troll will rip the idiot's arm from its—'

The ship juddered. On the table, Nils' glass wobbled, sloshing the remains of his beer. Nils stopped speaking, reached out an arm to steady himself.

'What the...'

A low grinding, scraping noise, like tearing metal, echoed through the bowels of the ship. All the tiny hairs rose on the back of Johan's neck.

'What the hell was *that*?' gasped Oskar, letting his opponent's arm drop.

An unnerving quiet had fallen on the *Titanic*.

Johan cocked his head, listening. He could hear the clock on the wall ticking, someone coughing in their cabin nearby, small sounds he'd never have been able to hear above the engines' constant roar.

'The engines have stopped.'

His voice sounded as wavery as an old man's.

Nils clicked his tongue. The fear Johan imagined he'd seen in his eyes, had been replaced by annoyance.

'I hope this ship hasn't broken down. I don't fancy being towed all the way to New York. It'll take weeks. My uncle's collecting me at the dock. He won't be happy if his journey home's delayed.'

There was a clattering of boots on metal. Heart racing, Johan spun round, convinced something terrible was happening.

A group of lads were hurtling down the steps. One of them, his face glowing with excitement, was yelling in Swedish.

'You won't believe what's happened! We've hit an iceberg! There are big lumps of ice all over the deck! Come and see!'

Johan snatched up his cap and was swept along in a wave of men, heading for the forward deck. When they surged through the doors, he saw that this wasn't the practical joke he'd suspected. The deck was littered with chunks and shards of ice, glittering like glass under the ship's bright lights.

Nils gave an excited yell and waved his arm.

'Look, there it is! An actual iceberg! Can you spot a polar bear?'

Johan followed Nils as he hurried over to the rail. He looked out into the ice-cold, starlit night. In the far distance, he could see a dark, lumpen shape, even blacker than the night sky. When he spoke, the freezing air burned his lungs.

'It doesn't look that impressive.'

Nils snorted.

'Maybe not, but most of its bulk will be below the water line. If we'd hit it head on, we'd have been in real trouble, I reckon.'

Johan remembered the terrible grinding sound.

'Do you think it has damaged the ship? Is that why the engines have stopped?'

'You're a right worrier, aren't you?' laughed Nils. 'We're on the *Titanic*. She's unsinkable, didn't you hear? Oi, Oskar, pass that ball!'

A huge lump of ice skittered across the deck, tiny particles flying in all directions, like shattering glass. Nils kicked the ice, with such force it shot skyward, and skidded off the end of the deck.

'I need another ball!' he yelled, and Olaf obliged. Within seconds, a noisy game of ice football had started. Johan joined in, acting as goalkeeper for the Swedes, when he wasn't creased with laughter at the jokes and daft antics of the others. To loud cheers, he saved an Irish goal by diving on top of the "*ball*" before it skittered under the railings, and he knew in his heart that he'd take the memory of this bizarre game of football to the grave.

It was terrific fun, but despite the exercise, the intense cold started to bite through Johan's clothes. He shivered, sticking his frozen hands under his jacket to warm them. Nils noticed.

'Come on, kiddo. We'd better get you back inside. Don't want you having a relapse.'

As the two of them made their way back down the steps, doubts began trickling into Johan's brain. What if the iceberg *had* torn a hole in the hull? *What if somewhere deep below, water was flooding into the ship?*

He opened his mouth to voice his doubts, but remembered Nil describing him as a worrier, and decided against it.

They were soon joined by the others. Oskar fell into a drunken stupor but the other three played cards for a while.

'Do you think they'll restart the engines soon?' asked Nils. 'I wouldn't like to think we were drifting miles off course.'

'That wouldn't be good,' sighed Olaf. 'I heard a steward say we're in the middle of an ice field. Imagine it. We're drifting through a sea of icebergs!'

It was an eerie thought, almost impossible to imagine. Surely a collision must be inevitable? Johan's body tensed, waiting for the bang, and when someone knocked on the cabin door, he jumped so hard his cards flew out of his hand and scattered across the floor.

'What's going on now?' wondered Nils, shoving his feet into his boots. 'Perhaps the football game got out of hand after we left. I hope there hasn't been trouble. I'll go and find out.'

But then a voice echoed down the passageway. Somebody yelled in Swedish, and Johan's heart turned to ice.

'Water's coming in! The ship's leaking like a sieve! Leave your cabins and get up on deck!'

Panic burst like a boil.

'Wake up, Oskar!' yelled Nils, shaking him. 'We need to go! Now!'

Nils threw the cabin door open and ran out, yelling at them all to follow. Oskar leapt from his top bunk. His ankle cracked against Johan's skull, and the boy fell backwards, dazed. He lay there, head swimming, listening to the thunder of boots tramping past. The men in the aft cabins must heading along Scotland Road, the crew's main passageway that stretched the length of the ship. As the dizziness faded, Johan staggered to his feet, struggling to think.

If the ship was sinking, he needed to get on a lifeboat. There were no lifeboats on the aft Well Deck where the other men were heading. All the lifeboats were on the Boat Deck, in 1st and 2nd Class. If he wanted to survive, that's where he needed to go.

And I do want to live. No matter how hard life is going to be on the farm, I don't want to die tonight. I want a happy life and a job I love and I'll make it happen eventually somehow. And who else will help my mother and little brothers get to America?

Johan shrugged on his jacket, and fixed his tie. But he didn't bother tying his laces, because as he was tugging on his boots, something terrifying happened. A river of water gushed into the cabin, flooding the floor, sending the playing cards spinning. For long, ticking seconds, Johan stood frozen to the spot while icy, dark green sea water surged round his boots, and the Queen of Hearts floated away, smiling serenely, but then adrenalin kicked in. Boot laces trailing in the ankle deep water, he rushed from the cabin. The corridor had become a fast-flowing river and the water levels seemed to be rising.

Chapter 17

Bertha

15th April 1912

Bertha!

Mother's voice, quiet, but urgent, broke through her dream.

'Bertha, wake up! We've got to get up and go on deck.'

She opened her eyes, groggy, her dream dissolving as reality encroached.

'What's happening? Is it morning?'

Her mother shook her head.

'No, it's just after midnight. Come along. There's no time to lose.'

Bertha threw off her blankets and clambered down from her bunk.

'Is it a drill?'

'It seems not. That's a good lass. Put your coat on over your nightie. It'll be freezing out there. No, leave your books, Bertha.'

Reluctantly, Bertha put down the stack of books she'd lifted from her trunk. It would be a dull wait up on deck with nothing to do.

'Where have I put my blue scarf? The very night I need it, and it's missing.'

Bertha gulped. She knew exactly where Mrs Pinsky's blue scarf was located. She'd forgotten to return it and, unless it had been nabbed by a deckhand, the scarf was still stuffed behind a bench on the Promenade Deck.

Giving up on the scarf, Rosa bundled herself in a plaid shawl.

'This is not what I paid for, when I bought my ticket,' she grumbled. 'Comfort and luxury, they told me.'

The shawl made Mrs Pinsky look like one of the fishwives who worked on the harbour at Peterhead, but it seemed rude to tell her, especially when her eyes were creased with anxiety.

And when Bertha glanced at her own reflection in the wardrobe mirror, she figured it would be pot calling the kettle black. Pale-faced, shadows under her eyes, dressed in a white cotton nightdress and with her hair in ratty tangles, she looked less than glamorous herself.

Rosa was still muttering away as she hauled a lifejacket over her head.

'I'm sure the brochure said the Titanic's *virtually unsinkable*. There was certainly no mention of lifeboats.'

Lifeboats!

Bertha remembered the lifeboats hanging from davits over the side of the ships. Imagine being lowered down in one of those tiny boats, in the middle of the night, into the deep, dark sea, miles below.

Her mother must have noticed Bertha's expression.

'Don't get wound up like a clockwork mouse, Bertha. Get your coat. Button it up to the neck and put on your hat.'

While Bertha fetched her hat and coat, she bumped into Ellen Toomey, who was bustling around the cramped cabin, loading her possessions into her carpet bag.

'Will you watch where you're going, child! I nearly dropped my rosary beads.'

'Pop the beads in your coat pocket and put the bag down, Ellen. They'll not let you take it.'

Bertha started at her mother's sharp tone. She noticed her mouth was a tight line, her face drawn. Panic fluttered like a moth in her chest, and she grabbed her mother's hand.

'What's wrong, Mother? Is this definitely not a drill?'

'No, I've told you already. They wouldn't consider having a drill on such a cold night as this one. They're having trouble of some kind.'

She plonked Bertha's lifejacket over her head. It was heavy, awkward and uncomfortable, but wearing it made her feel safer. At least if she fell out of the lifeboat into the sea she wouldn't sink under the waves. With all the cork in this lifejacket she'd bob around in the water for ages. And she was quite good at swimming. Her back stroke was particularly strong. Mind you, they must be some distance from land. She opened her mouth to ask how far, but Rosa Pinsky spoke first.

'Who told you there was trouble, Bessie?' she asked, her plump fingers trembling as she struggled to fasten her own lifejacket. 'Did the steward knock? I didn't hear him.'

Mother shook her head. While she buckled Bertha into her lifejacket, she told the others what she knew.

'I couldn't sleep, so was reading by lamplight when I heard a loud sound, rather like crashing glass, or marbles rolling across a baking tin. I threw on my dressing gown, and went up on deck to investigate.

There were lots of people milling around, which seemed odd when it was so late. I saw Captain Smith, Mr Ismay and Mr Andrews, all wearing very glum expressions. They were in deep conversation, and I didn't feel I should approach them, so I marched up to an officer and asked him what the matter was. He said very firmly that there was nothing wrong and I should go straight back to bed.

There was something shifty in his expression though, and I knew he was lying, but wasn't sure what to do next. I was about to head back downstairs, when Mr Collyer approached me, quite shaken. He pointed out to sea, at this dark shape, which I could hardly believe I hadn't noticed. And he told me we'd hit an iceberg. I asked if all was well, and he shook his head, and whispered that he'd just seen a first class lifeboat being lowered. He took my hand, insisted I should go and collect my little girl and get up on deck. Before I scurried off, he said we should put our life jackets on, and I think we'd be wise to heed his advice.

Mr Collyer does not seem the type of person to cause an unnecessary alarm. He has spoken to Mr Norman who is going to fetch Kate Buss and he'll tell young Dr Pain to collect Marion.'

Bertha's heart began to thud against her ribs.

'But what about everyone else? Aren't they going to get on to the lifeboats too? What about the crew? And little Lolo and Momon? What about Reginald?'

She blushed, embarrassed that she'd singled out the lift boy, but her mother was too busy batting Bertha's worries aside to even notice.

'They'll put us all into lifeboats, you'll see, just to be on the safe side. It'll be fine, Bertha, I promise. Please don't worry. Chins up, ladies. Let's go.'

As they lumbered out of the cabin, awkward in the heavy life jackets, Bertha's stomach lurched, reluctant to voice the questions preying on her mind.

If the ship has really hit an iceberg, if the crew are already lowering the lifeboats filled with 1st Class passengers, why did the steward tell you to go back to bed? Is it because there isn't enough room on the lifeboats for everyone?

Fear prickled her insides, as she thought of the stokers deep down in the engine room, of Reginald trapped at his post, of Johan in his 3rd Class cabin on E-Deck. She hoped they all had a Mr Collyer to tell them what was going on, and were heading up to the lifeboats. She prayed they were not being told by the stewards that there was nothing the matter, and that they should go back to bed.

Because there was something terribly wrong, she could feel it. For the first time, she'd become aware of that the steady thrum of the engines had stopped, and the absence of sound was chilling.

But there were other noises, a clattering of feet on the stairway, a rumble of raised voices outside in the passageway. Her mother ushered her along the corridor, up the stairs. As she climbed, Bertha had the strangest feeling that the ship was slightly off kilter, and that they were tipping forward as they climbed. Fear made her hands clammy, her mouth dry.

When she walked outside, on to the Boat Deck, the shock of the cold made her gasp. She could hardly hear what people were saying because of the noise, a harsh, deafening screech.

'What's that dreadful noise?' she asked, huddling against the warm tweed of her mother's coat.

'I asked Mr Collyer the same thing. He said that it's high-pressure steam venting from the boilers. Just like on a locomotive. It's nothing to worry about.'

'What's happening?' asked Ellen Toomey, staring around, eyes frantic. 'What are our instructions?'

'We need to wait, Ellen.' Mother's tone was crisp. 'And we need to stay calm. Panicking will help nobody. Take deep, calming breaths. Imagine we're picnicking in a wheat field.'

Ellen looked at Bertha's mother as if she were crazy, but Bertha felt a little comforted. There wasn't a trace of fear in her mother's voice. If her mother could be this brave, so could she. She looked around, trying to make sense of the scene on the deck.

There didn't seem to be any panic, but people were milling around, clearly unsure what to do. The Boat Deck was cluttered with abandoned bags and cases, which made crossing it an obstacle course. Families huddled, mothers clutching children, young couples clinging to one another. Some were weeping; others looked thoroughly annoyed to have been disturbed from their sleep. The vast majority appeared to be 1st or 2nd Class passengers, and few of them were properly dressed for the weather. Some of the ladies were shivering in silk evening gowns and many, like Bertha, were wearing coats over nightclothes and slippers.

'They refused to let me collect my jewellery case from the Purser's Office,' she heard a lady complain. 'It's a disgrace. I shall explain to the White Star Line in the strongest possible terms when we reach New York.'

For what seemed like an hour, but might only have been a few minutes, Bertha and the three women stood, frozen, with no idea where to go or what to do, waiting for instructions which didn't come. She saw the Collyers, and shouted for Madge, who didn't hear her, and no wonder, because the orchestra had set up on deck and had begun to play jaunty tunes, which fought to be heard over the frantic screeching from the ship's boilers.

'Lower away!'

An officer shouted, the deckhands got to work, and another lifeboat, less than half full, was lowered over the port side of the ship. Mother held Bertha close and looked right and left, trying to weigh up their options.

'There's Officer Murdoch. He's a Scot. He'll know what's going on. Come this way.'

Stumbling in her slippers, the icy air slicing at her bare legs, Bertha hurried across the deck, the other ladies following, towards the starboard side.

When a projectile whizzed into the air, followed by a deafening bang, Bertha ducked, afraid that the *Titanic* was breaking apart.

When she looked up, a great shower of white stars was cascading from the sky. She screwed up her face, baffled.

'Why are they setting off fireworks now?'

Her mother gave her hand a squeeze.

'The Captain is firing distress rockets, in the hope that another ship will see them and come immediately to our rescue. There are bound to be several in the vicinity.'

She sounded completely convincing, but Bertha couldn't help wondering if her mother's unruffled exterior was for her benefit.

Was panic bubbling up in her mother's chest, the way it was in her own?

Chapter 18

Johan

15th April 1912

At first, Johan was so disorientated by the bang on his head, and so shocked by the rush of freezing water which slapped against his calves, that it was impossible to come up with a plan. This was such a terrifying scenario, that his first instinct was to head up Scotland Road, because at least if he followed the others, he wouldn't be alone when this ship began to sink, as it surely must. But—if he wanted on a lifeboat—he couldn't stay in 3rd Class. He had to reach the Boat Deck.

He looked up and down the corridor, wondering if all those cabins were empty, afraid some folk might be fast asleep while the water rose around their bunks. Shivering with cold, he waded through the rising grey-green water, trying to block out the horrifying realisation that the ocean was flooding into the *Titanic*. He banged on doors, shouting until he was hoarse, but nobody answered. He began to fear that he was alone down there; that he was going to drown or freeze to death, deep in the bowels of the ship. His teeth were chattering, and the cold numbed his limbs. Frantic, he tried to think of the quickest escape route.

The crew used Scotland Road for transporting goods and equipment the length of the ship. They also used access ladders to get up and down quickly. In this scenario, upwards was the only direction that made sense.

The nearest ladder was some distance away and by the time he reached it, the surging water was almost waist deep, and he was so cold his bones ached. As he grabbed the bottom rung, the freezing metal burned his fingers, and a memory swept over him, of the long ago winter's day when some older boys had dared him to take off his mittens and touch a railing, and then stood roaring with laughter when his hand had stuck to the icy metal. He'd been left with a red raw patch of skin on his palm, and his mother had gone hunting for the boys, waving his grandfather's walking stick like a weapon.

But this wasn't a stupid dare. This was a matter of life or death. He tried to ignore the painful sting in his fingers, and started to climb steadily, hand over hand, ever upwards. Between D and C Deck his progress was halted by two small figures up ahead, taking the same route to safety, but moving agonisingly slowly. They looked down at him, dark eyes round with fear, and he recognised them as 3rd Class passengers, a young Lebanese lad and his little sister. When he called to them to hurry up and get a move on, he knew they wouldn't understand, and feared they'd all die, frozen with fear on this iron ladder.

But his firm tone seemed to do the trick, and they moved faster, though the poor girl was impeded by her long skirt. Why was female clothing so impractical, he wondered, when in his experience, and he guessed in these children's too, women worked as hard as men? It didn't seem at all sensible—or fair.

As he reached the top of the ladder leading to the Forward Well Deck, he found the two children waiting for him, the boy's arm round his little sister's shoulders, and guessed what was wrong. The next ladder led them into forbidden territory. But their lives now depended on them breaking the rules. So he pointed upwards towards the Bridge Deck and gestured at them to follow him. As Johan climbed, an uncomfortable thought buzzed in his brain. The ladders were meant to be vertical, leading ever upwards to the Boat Deck. But something terrible was happening on this ship. It was tilting, dipping forward, as if it was about to dive underwater.

Finally, he reached the top of the final ladder, and he hauled the boy up the last few rungs, helped his sobbing sister up too. He scurried across the Bridge and scanned the Boat Deck.

It was a peculiar, unsettling scene: people standing in clusters, some wearing worried expressions, some annoyed. A man in evening dress was laughing, a loud bray like a donkey's. He clearly hadn't seen what Johan had seen, down on the lower decks, had no idea that the ship was filling with seawater.

As they scrambled down the steps onto the Boat Deck, Johan first heard the words that would haunt him for the next terrible hour:

Women and children first!

A well-dressed man picked the Lebanese girl up and threw her onto the nearest lifeboat. Her brother scrambled on too, but when Johan tried to join them, he was held back by an officer.

'Didn't you hear? Women and children first, you coward!'

A deckhand shoved him in the chest, so hard he skidded on his back across the deck, crashing against a bench. Winded, he lay for a moment, taking deep, gasping breaths of air so frigid it stung his lungs.

Then he got up, using the bench as support, and stared around, desperate to see a familiar face, someone who could help him make sense of what was happening. The ship he was on was sinking, and he wasn't being allowed to leave.

Everyone seemed to be British or American; the 3rd Class passengers were where he'd feared they'd be, crowded behind the gate on the aft Well Deck. As he watched, some young lads pushed an officer out of

156

the way, and launched themselves over the gate. They headed straight for an empty lifeboat on the starboard side of the ship, and when they reached it, started to drag off its tarpaulin. His heart drumming against his ribs, Johan ran over to join them.

Chapter 19

Bertha

15th April 1912

As if sensing her doubts, Bertha's mother let go of her hand.

'Your hands are cold as ice, dear. Give them a vigorous rub; it will get your circulation going. Oh, look! There are Marion and Kate at last!'

Her mother's voice was as cheerful as if the two women had arrived for afternoon tea. 'And thank heavens, Mr Norman and Doctor Pain are with them. We shall all board a lifeboat together. What an adventure it will be. Coo-ee! Over here!'

Herding together, shepherded by Bertha's mother, they all headed towards Officer Murdoch. As they approached, Bertha could sense that the atmosphere on deck was beginning to change and could see her own fear reflected in adult faces. Several lifeboats had already been lowered. It must be clear to everybody with eyes that there were a limited number of spaces left. The decks were now thronging with people, and at the gate that led up from the Well Deck, a crowd of 3rd Class passengers had gathered. Officers were trying to hold those people back, telling them they couldn't get through, and that these were restricted areas.

'Look at the silly creatures, hoping to get on lifeboats laden with luggage!' sneered a passing lady.

To Bertha's astonishment, mild Kate Buss reacted with fury.

'Have you considered that the luggage they're carrying might be all those poor souls have in the world! And how can they get on lifeboats, when the stewards aren't letting them pass?'

The lady looked affronted.

'It's only right that we have priority, when we paid a fortune for our tickets!' she snapped.

Looking at the faces of the people crammed behind the gate to the Well Deck, a shiver ran up Bertha's spine. She could tell by the terror in their eyes that they knew something terrible had happened. And their escape was being blocked because some people considered their lives were more important.

As they approached the railings, Bertha could hear Murdoch and another officer bawling instructions to the crewmen launching a lifeboat. To Bertha's utter disbelief, the lifeboat contained only a dozen people, more than half of them crew.

'Mother, why are there so few people on that boat? There are so many people on this ship; shouldn't the lifeboats be full before they're launched?'

'I expect the lifeboat will stop on the lower decks to allow more people to get on, dear. I am sure the officers know exactly what they're doing.'

They certainly weren't giving that impression, from the bellowed instructions and the anxiety etched on their faces. The crewmen they were yelling at didn't appear to be at all familiar with handling the boat gear. It all seemed alarmingly clumsy and haphazard.

As the lifeboat was launched, a woman screamed in terror, and tried to scramble out. Watching her panic, Bertha's stomach churned. She didn't think she could bear to get into one of those little boats and be lowered down the side of the ship, into that black, glistening sea. But if the ship was sinking, what choice did she have? She turned, scanned the decks, and spotted Mr Hoffman. The boys were huddled by his side, and he was buttoning them into cosy chinchilla coats. Mr Hoffman's face was a mask of anxiety. He kept glancing towards the deckhouse as if he was considering taking the children back downstairs. She wanted to call out to him, tell him to stay out on deck, that he mustn't risk the little boys' lives.

She couldn't see Madge or her parents any longer, and there was no sign of Johan. She prayed he wasn't fast asleep in his cabin, because if he was, what fate awaited him? And what about Reginald? Would he be allowed on a lifeboat, or be expected to stay in the lift, even as the ship sank? It was a terrifying thought.

'*Women and children first, you cowards!*'

In one hand, First Officer Murdoch was gripping the thick rope which attached a lifeboat to its davits—in the other he was waving a pistol. Bertha's mother stepped back in alarm, trying to shield Bertha behind her tweed coat. But Bertha could see what was happening. This lifeboat was already full. Again, Murdoch roared at the men who were crouching in the bottom of the boat.

'Get your carcasses out of there, or I'll throw you all overboard myself!'

Shouting and cursing, the group of young men scrambled out of the lifeboat. To Bertha's horror, she realised that one of them was Johan. He looked at her and she saw fear flicker across his face. She reached out her hand, heartbroken for him. He deserved a place in the boat as much as she did. He was only a boy. She opened her mouth to tell Murdoch, but it was too late. Johan had gone, running off to the other side of the ship.

As soon as the lifeboat had been emptied, First Officer Murdoch began to call for any women and children standing nearby to get aboard. Bertha froze in terror.

'I can't,' she whispered.

Her mother gave her a none too gentle shove.

'Indeed you can, and you must. Set a good example to the others.'

It was as terrifying as Bertha had imagined, stepping on to a tiny boat, swinging so high above a pitch-black sea. Once inside, she sat on a bench and held on so tight her knuckles turned white.

'Women and children first!' roared Murdoch again, and all the waiting ladies clambered one at a time into the lifeboat. A man hurried over and threw a young lady aboard, ignoring her shrieks and pleas to be allowed to stay on the ship.

As he strode away, her wails intensified, and she tried to scramble out.

'Come with me, Ben! Don't leave me!'

Bertha's mother clicked her tongue disapprovingly.

'You need to stop that nonsense. You're frightening my child.'

'Listen to the woman. Calm yourself, Ninette,' sighed the lady's maid, pulling at the hem of her skirt. 'Ben will get on the next lifeboat, I'm sure. Please sit down, before you tip us all into the sea.'

As she put two and two together, Ellen gave a horrified gasp, and drew her rosary beads from her pocket.

'That's Ben Gugenheim's floozy,' she muttered, fingering the beads, as if they'd protect her from the scandal. 'I hope she doesn't sit anywhere near *me*.'

As if endeavouring to annoy Ellen, Ninette plonked herself on the bench opposite, where she clung to her maid and wept that she'd had to leave all her jewellery behind.

'I've had to leave my son behind, so pipe down,' snapped a woman.

Once the ladies were seated, Murdoch allowed several crew members to get aboard, and a few male passengers jumped on too. The men sat hunched, hats pulled low, as if terrified they'd be noticed and ordered off the boat.

Bertha knew the young men from the Dining Saloon. But Mr Norman and Doctor Pain, who had helped the ladies to board, were now standing back, making no attempt to get on the lifeboat.

Bertha's mother stood up in the boat, causing it to sway wildly on its ropes. Ninette screamed like a banshee, but Bessie Watt ignored her and kept her eyes fixed on the two young men.

'Come along. Please, get on,' she insisted. 'Look, the stamp says this boat has the capacity to hold seventy people, and there's less than forty on board. You must get on. Your poor mothers...'

'Sit down, ma'am! We're lowering the boat!' called Murdoch. He gestured to the deckhands and the boat jerked. Ninette Aubart gave a barn owl screech and clutched at her maid.

Bertha's mother flopped down on to a bench, her face stricken.

'I expect you were right in what you said earlier, Bessie. They'll stop at the lower decks and let more women and children on board,' said Mrs Pinsky. 'After all, there are no lifeboats in the 3rd Class areas, so they must have an alternative means of escape. Mustn't they?'

But the crew didn't stop. They were lowered jerkily, terrifyingly, downwards, past each brightly lit deck.

Bertha's mother sat ramrod straight, but when Bertha glanced up, she saw a single tear glittering on the woman's cheek.

'Mr Norman and Doctor Pain should have got on the boat.' Bertha's tone was indignant. 'There's plenty of room. Look, some of these ladies have their feet up on the seats!'

Her mother brushed the tear from her face and stared ahead at the star-dusted sky.

'Our menfolk are following established rules, Bertha, about how gentlemen should conduct themselves in emergencies. They won't attempt to save themselves when women and children are still aboard the ship. And I admire their courage, truly I do, but there are 30 odd spaces on this lifeboat and it grieves me that 30 precious souls have just been sacrificed for no good reason.'

Bertha shivered, as she realised what her mother had just said.

'The *Titanic* can't sink. She's meant to be unsinkable,' she whispered.

Her mother didn't reply, but as their descent momentarily ceased, she pointed towards a porthole. As Bertha stared inside the ship, she saw an armchair bob past the window, carried along on a dark, surging tide.

When their boat hit the water, Ninette screamed again, a horrible sound which cut the darkness like a knife. The boat lurched and Bertha slipped forwards in her seat, but was tugged back up by her mother.

'There's a lot of water swirling around in the bottom of this boat. Tuck your knees up, so your feet are off the floor. You mustn't let your slippers get wet. That's the girl. Wrap your coat round them. Isn't it lucky we bought that coat with growth-room?'

Bertha did as she was told. The night air was frigid. Intense cold pierced her lungs with every breath and she wished she had a warm shawl like Mrs Pinsky's to cover her face.

Her mother put an arm round her shoulders and Bertha buried herself in the warmth of her tweed coat, breathing in her mother's lavender scent as the little boat bobbed like a cork on the water, which had seemed as smooth as glass from the deck of the *Titanic*.

A man stood up in the boat, grabbing for the oars.

'We need to get the boat clear of the ship. When she goes down, the suction will take us with her.'

One of the older women began to wail.

'No, no, no! She can't go down! My husband and son are on board!'

'Hush now.' Mother's voice was quiet, soothing, as if she was speaking to a small child. 'He meant *if* the ship goes down, not when.' Then she called out. 'I can row, if you need another pair of hands.'

Bertha tightened her grip on her mother. 'Stay here with me,' she pleaded, ashamed of her clinginess, but too overwhelmed with fear to bear the thought of being alone.

Her mother's voice in the darkness was kind, but firm. 'If this were a nice night on Loch Ness, we'd just be out for a row. Look how calm the water is, and how brightly the stars are twinkling. We'll be fine, dear. You and I will not drown tonight, I swear it.'

She took a set of oars, and started rowing, keeping in rhythm with the crew. As the boat skimmed through the water, heading away from the stricken ship, Bertha's mother began to sing. Bertha tried to equal her mother's bravery, wiping the tears from her eyes with her sleeve, hugging herself tight to stop her body from trembling. But when she tried to sing along to *Speed Bonnie Boat*, the words died in her throat. Because when she looked back at the *Titanic*, it looked much lower in the water than it had been minutes earlier, and the bow seemed to be tipping into the sea. As she stared, another row of lights went out.

Chapter 20

Johan

15th April 1912

There was full scale panic on deck now. Johan's lungs felt like they were going to burst, as he raced from starboard to port, where Lifeboat 12 was being lowered. He reached the railings and swung a leg over, planning to leap into the boat, but was dragged back by an officer, who roared in his face, and threw him backwards, leaving him sprawled like a starfish on the deck.

The offices were behaving as if trying to save yourself from drowning was a crime. He kept hearing the same shout, and wished he could puzzle out its meaning.

Women and children first!

If he could figure it out, maybe he might be able to understand why the crew wouldn't let him save his own life.

By the time Johan had run back over to the starboard side, yet another lifeboat was being lowered, but this one was crammed with people, and he could see there was no chance of being allowed aboard. Hope was beginning to fizzle out. The deck was tilting to port, and with the lower decks flooded, he felt in his bones that the *Titanic* was in its death throes.

Clutching the railings, Johan looked over the side. The ship's lights still shone, although there seemed to be fewer of them. Their reflections glimmered on the sea, which seemed to be getting ever closer—but it was still terrifyingly far down. Could he jump? Or would he be sucked under into the giant bronze propellers? And even if he could swim away from the ship, how long could he survive in that freezing water?

The second last lifeboat was filled to bursting. People had realised the danger they were in, and were fighting for a place. The officers fired warning shots, in a hopeless effort to retain control in a dreadful situation. As Murdoch roared for the boat to be lowered, it dipped below the rail, disappearing from Johan's view, beginning its dizzying journey towards the Atlantic Ocean.

Tears trickled down Johan's face, as he tried to face the unbearable. He was going to die tonight after all.

'Well, well. The little thief.'

As he spun to face the familiar voice, panic flared in Johan's chest. The red-haired stoker stood beside him at the railing, his face washed clean of coal dust, dark blood flowing from a nasty gash on his arm.

'But I guess all that doesn't matter a jot now. We're both dead men, and there's no point taking a quarrel to the grave.'

In the shadows, the stoker's rueful smile looked a sinister grimace, and Johan took a step away from him. The stoker glanced over the railings, and then back at Johan. He ran a hand through his shock of red hair.

'You're just a wee lad. If you're going to get on that boat, you'll need to jump.'

The stoker stepped towards Johan, pointing down at the lifeboat, making its jerky descent.

'The weight of me would tip that lot into the water, but a lad like you will make no difference. Go on, jump, you wee eejit!'

The stoker pushed Johan hard in the back. Panicking, sure that the man was about to beat him senseless, or throw him into the ship's propeller, Johan scrambled over the railing, and leapt into the darkness. He closed his eyes, waiting for the splash, and the shock of freezing water closing over his head.

But the lifeboat had stopped at A Deck to pick up more passengers. Johan didn't fall far, but he did land heavily, right on top of a plump lady in an ostrich feather hat. She squealed, and pushed him hard. As he lay, like an upended crab in the bottom of the boat, he saw the stoker looking down at him. The man waved and gave him a thumbs up, and finally Johan understood.

But he wasn't out of danger yet.

Water was flooding into the lifeboat, spewing out the side of the ship from the exhaust of Titanic's condensers, soaking the woman's ridiculous hat, filling the space where he lay in the bottom of the boat. Johan struggled to his feet, and saw to his horror, that the force of the water was pushing their boat towards the stern, directly underneath the next lifeboat, which was crammed with passengers and crew, and descending on top of them, about to crush all those aboard.

Everyone on Lifeboat 13 started screaming.

'Stop lowering! *Stop! You're going to kill us all!*'

But they couldn't be heard above the screams on the deck, the screech of escaping steam, and the terrible creaks and groans of the dying ship.

One of the crewmen leapt up, whipped out a knife and began to slash at the ropes tethering the lifeboat. Johan ducked down in the freezing water, desperate to avoid being crushed by the boat which was inching towards them.

There were gasps of relief, followed by shrieks of fear, when the crewman sliced through the last rope, and the boat fell suddenly, splashing into the water, sending everyone flying in all directions. Johan's jaw crashed against one of the benches, but his relief was so intense, he was hardly aware of the pain. They were free of the stricken ship, and of Lifeboat 15. The deluge of water from the condensers was now pushing them towards the stern, and the crew snatched up oars and began to row away from the *Titanic*. Johan looked upwards, straining his eyes to see the red-haired stoker, wanting somehow to thank him for saving his life, but the people on *Titanic*'s deck looked as tiny as ants.

As the crewmen rowed away from the ship, Johan kept his eyes fixed on the *Titanic*. She was going down, there was no doubt about that. Her bow was underwater and as Johan watched, eyes round with disbelief, the stern of the ship began to rise out of the sea. As terrified screams cut the air, Johan crouched in the boat, shivering with horror, but unable to tear his eyes away, as hundreds of people clung frantically to railings, before letting go and sliding, crashing, tumbling, and screaming into the sea.

As *Titanic*'s front funnel came crashing down, the ship seemed to split in the middle. With a series of massive booms she plunged into the water, leaving no trace. And then came the sounds that would haunt Johan forever: the terrible sound of hundreds of men, women and children wailing. There was no room on their lifeboat, he could see that, but some of those lifeboats had been launched half empty. Surely many of the poor souls in the water would be saved? But the wails went on and on, until gradually the terrible sounds faded, and he could only hear the quiet sobs of a bereaved woman on the lifeboat and the groans of a badly injured crewman.

For hours he sat hunched, sodden wet and stiff with cold, in the bottom of Lifeboat 13. Now that the lights of *Titanic* had gone out for ever, he kept his eyes on the stars, glittering diamond-bright, trying to keep his mind off the horror below. But when dawn started to break, there was no escaping it. Only a handful of people had been plucked from the ocean by those on the *Titanic's* lifeboats and no ships had come to their rescue. The survivors were drifting in an icefield, surrounded by massive bergs, and facing the terrible sight of hundreds of frozen bodies, floating, almost upright in their lifejackets.

For a while, it appeared a similar fate could be in store all aboard Lifeboat 13. It was so low in the water that a girl's long hair was trailing in the water like seaweed. However hard they bailed, the bottom of the boat kept filling up.

But then a shout went up.

'*A ship! I see a ship!*'

At first, the survivors were reluctant to hope, but its lights gleamed bright in the grey dawn light, and it was soon clear that the ship was heading towards them. They were some distance away and had a long row back, but the crew tried to keep spirits up and sang all the way.

By early morning, everyone aboard Lifeboat 13 was on board the RMS *Carpathia*, wrapped in blankets, issued with soup and hot toddies. When one of *Carpathia's* passengers put her own shawl round his shivering shoulders, the act of kindness was too much. He flopped down on a bench, and for the first time since the nightmare began, Johan cried.

'Son, I think we've put you on the wrong deck.'

The steward's face was kindly enough, but he had a firm grip on Johan's shoulder. 'I think you belong in steerage, eh, lad?'

Frightened, Johan pulled away from him.

The steward pointed to a set of stairs.

'*Svenka*, down there.'

Johan nodded. They were putting him back in his place. Nothing had changed. But as he was led towards the steps, he felt glad to go, to get away from all those weeping women in their furs and nightdresses and ridiculous hats. Why were they grieving, when they'd refused to go back for their men? They'd been pitiless last night, when they'd rowed away and left them, screaming for help, freezing to death. He couldn't get the sound of those screams out of his head, and knew it would haunt his nightmares for the rest of his life. But despite that knowledge, he was glad he'd survived. He was thankful to be alive.

Just before he reached the steps, he glanced to the right and saw a face he recognised. It was Bertha, white faced, lank-haired, clutching her soup mug as if it was saving her life. She was staring out to sea, and didn't notice him being escorted back to steerage.

And then he saw someone else, and his heart broke. One of those little boys from the gate; the older one with the dark hair, was sitting on a bench, wailing, and clinging like a limpet to an elderly woman. The fair one, the toddler who'd reminded him of Gosta, was nowhere to be seen.

He trailed down the stairs, into the steerage areas. Oskar was there, standing at the rail, grief etched on his face. There was no sign of either Nils or Olaf. Far too many of the familiar faces from 3rd Class were missing. Johan walked up and down the silent, haunted deck, his eyes raking each face, searching, on a quest of his own.

Chapter 21

Bertha

16th—18th April

For two days, Bertha huddled in a deck chair in the *Carpathia*'s passenger lounge, unable to move. Faces kept flickering in front of her eyes, a long line of dead, queuing up to be remembered. Captain Smith, Mr Andrews, Mr Norman, Dr Pain, Mr Collyer... all those poor brave men, who'd stood aside and let the women and children board the lifeboats.

Had they known they were going to die? It was dreadful to imagine their terror as the ship upended, and plunged like a knife into the ocean, but she couldn't stop her brain from imagining it.

And it wasn't only the 2nd Class passengers she'd known who'd lost their lives. So many of the little children from 3rd Class that she'd seen running about on the Well Deck, so many of the passengers and crew, Reginald the lift boy... little Momon. There were too many dead to count.

Helpless tears trickled down her cheeks, as she remembered Momon's sweet smile, the softness of his curls. Mr Hoffman had gone down with the ship, but she felt more anger than grief towards him. She couldn't understand why he had waited until the last minute to put Lolo in one of the fragile collapsible lifeboats, or why he'd let Momon die, when all around him the crew had been yelling for children to be brought forward. Bertha could see Lolo now, toddling around the Passenger Lounge, watched over by kindly Mrs Hays, who spoke excellent French. She knew she should go over and help, but her legs seemed to have turned to jelly, and she couldn't summon the energy even to go and give the poor little orphan a hug.

Her mother's voice cut through her misery.

'Come on, Bertha. Up you get.'

Bertha shook her head, and cooried deeper into the blanket. For the last forty eight hours, her mother had spun like a dervish, comforting the bereaved, organising sewing bees, finding translators for those who couldn't speak English. If this experience had taught Bertha anything, it was that she had completely underestimated her mother. Even polar explorers and pioneering aviators would struggle to be as courageous and resourceful as Bessie Watt. Bertha was well aware now that she'd had an excellent role model right under her nose, but her desire for adventure had been snuffed out. All she wanted was somewhere quiet to sit and grieve.

'Come along, Bertha. Get up, right now. I've sewn a

couple of skirts from a ship's blanket, so at least you'll not arrive in New York in your nightie. Pop this one on, and then go and give the other to Marjorie. Look, it says RMS *Carpathia* along the hem. I'll bet a skirt like that will be all the rage in New York.'

Bertha shook her head, and tugged the blanket almost over her head. How could her mother make jokes, when so many people had died? What right did they have to be alive, when so many were dead?

'I don't want to see Madge. I just want to sit here, until we can get off this boat and Daddy can come and take us home.'

'You'll do no such thing. You've moped around long enough.'

Her mother's voice was so sharp that more tears sprang in Bertha's eyes. Her mother crouched down by her side, took one of Bertha's cold hands in her own, and rubbed it gently.

'I don't mean to be harsh, Bertha, but we're the lucky ones on this boat. Look up, look around at all those poor souls. So many have lost precious loved ones. Mrs Herman has lost her husband *and* her son. Mrs Abbott has lost *both* of her beloved sons. I am here with you, and your daddy is safely in Oregon.'

'I know that. And I want to be in Oregon too. I don't ever want to go on a boat again.'

Bertha's mother smiled, and shook her head.

'Well, I want us to visit my brother in Boston as we originally planned, and we're going to do it by boat. I'll not have you spend the rest of your life afraid of the water. We've survived, Bertha dear, while almost one thousand, five hundred souls have not. And we need to be thankful and we need to make the most of our lives— not bury ourselves in sadness and lethargy. Now, go and see your friend. She needs you.'

At first, moving felt too hard, but once she was out on deck, the chill wind skelped her face, bringing her back to life. Even so, as Bertha walked along the deck of the *Carpathia*, she had a strange sense of being somewhere haunted. Thin strands of mist fluttered like torn banners over the sea; far ahead, lights glimmered eerily through the fog. Huddled in deckchairs, women, faces etched with sadness, were silent as wraiths. Even the children were subdued, grieving their lost fathers.

She saw Madge, sitting alone on a bench, looking a world away from the adored only child she'd first met, the sweet girl with the ringlets, china doll and bright eyed smile. Now, her hair hung in limp, unwashed tangles, and she wore a torn, stained nightdress under her coat.

When Bertha called her name, Madge looked up. The heartbreak in her eyes was so deep, it finally dawned on Bertha that she was merely splashing in its shallows.

'My mother's made you a skirt,' she said, holding up the hideous garment. 'I know it looks awful, but it's quite cosy. I'll help you put it on, if you like.'

Madge stood, rigid and silent by the bench, while Bertha tugged the skirt over her legs, and tucked her nightdress under the waistband. When Madge finally spoke her voice was dull, leeched of all colour.

'When I was in the lifeboat with Mummy, I was worried sick about Dolly.' She slumped on to the bench and picked at the pleats of her handmade skirt. 'I imagined her sinking under the waves, wet and cold, crying for help...'

The wind was whipping Madge's hair across her face, but she seemed oblivious.

'I thought Daddy was safe. I thought he was on another lifeboat.'

Her voice cracked and a tear trickled down her cheek.

'She thinks I don't know that Daddy's dead, because she doesn't know I'm a detective and can read all the clues. I'm pretending I think there's hope, so Mummy doesn't give up.'

She began to cry, her whole body shuddering with sobs. Bertha glanced around, hands flapping in desperation, wishing her mother would magically appear and make things better. But nobody came, and Madge's sobs were becoming terrible animal howls.

'Don't cry, Madge. Please, don't cry,' she pleaded, hugging her tight, stroking her matted hair, until, after what seemed like forever, Madge's wails ceased, and she huddled quietly in Bertha's arms. They sat together, watching the grey fog drift across the ocean as the *Carpathia* skimmed towards New York.

'I need to go to my mother. She needs me,' said Madge finally, getting to her feet and wiping the tears from her eyes. 'All our money was in Papa's wallet and all our possessions were in the Purser's Office. We have nothing left, and my mother isn't strong. But we will get to Idaho, all by ourselves, and we will plant the fruit trees and grow peaches and plums. The sunshine will make her well again, you'll see.'

'I'll come and visit,' Bertha smiled at her, desperate to bring sunshine back to Madge's face. 'And we will have a glorious picnic in your orchard. Then I'll take you for a spin in my brand new airplane.'

Madge's eyes were fierce.

'This isn't pretend, Bertha. It's real life.'

Bertha didn't drop her eyes. She looked straight into Madge's, and willed her story to be true.

'It *is* real life, Madge. It will definitely happen. We can have apple crumble at the picnic, if you like.'

'Pork pies too. And jam tarts.'

'Oh, definitely jam tarts. Goes without saying.'

Madge flung her arms round Bertha's neck.

'You're the best friend I ever had. I wish...'

She didn't finish, just stood up and walked away, her new skirt flapping almost to her ankles.

Bertha sat on the bench, chewing on her lip, her tears mixing with the drizzle.

She'd overheard her own mother and Marion talking last night, and Marion's words were echoing in her head.

Poor Charlotte Collyer will never manage in Idaho alone. She'd be better to go home, back to her own folks.

Then a voice called her name.

'Robertta!'

Whipping round, her hand flew to her mouth. Johan was waving at her from behind a pillar, and the sight brought so many memories flooding into her brain that she was left breathless; reminded of treasure maps, mysteries, and *The Collyer-Watt Detective Agency*. Those exciting days before tragedy struck seemed another world away.

As she walked towards Johan, she realised he wasn't alone, but was holding the hand of a tiny, fair-haired child. She ran towards them, yelling, her voice cracking.

'Momon! You've found Momon!'

Gathering the toddler up in her arms, she squeezed him tight, loving the warmth and cuddly weight of him. Johan hung back, leaning nonchalantly against the pillar, as if all this was no big deal. But when Bertha looked up, and their eyes met, she saw tears glistening in his eyes too. Then he beamed at her, his smile as proud as Punch.

'*Jag hittade skatten.*'

She recognised a word, and nodded.

'You found treasure.'

Putting Momon carefully down on the bench, she threw her arms round Johan's neck and hugged him.

'Thank you, Johan. Thank you so very, very much.'

She released him, and pulled the photograph from her coat pocket. It was slightly water stained and curled at the edges, but the faces of the couple and their little girl were still intact.

'You've reunited those little boys. And I've kept little Alice's photograph safe. I'll post it to Francis as soon as I set foot in New York.'

She stuffed the photo back in her pocket, wiping the tears from her face.

'We can't turn back time, Johan, but we must do the best we can with our lives now. We owe it to the people who died, so we could live.'

She wasn't sure if he understood or not, or even if she was talking to him at all, or to herself, but she knew in her heart that what she was saying was true, and that Johan knew it too.

Epilogue

Bertha

May 1912

When Bertha opened the window, a warm breeze made her gingham curtains flutter. She waved at her father, who was busy polishing his pride and joy, a Racycle Roadster.

'Morning, Daddy!'

'Afternoon more like, lazybones! I've already been out for a spin while you've been in the Land of Nod.'

Bertha watched as her father unlocked the shed, and carefully pushed his bicycle inside.

He rode it to work in Portland every weekday morning, although he'd need to start using the horse and buggy when Bertha started Jefferson High in September. The thought of school made Bertha both excited and nervous in equal measure. The local girls she'd met so far seemed perfectly nice, but they treated her more as a minor celebrity than a potential new friend—they were as keen as the reporters to interview an actual Titanic survivor.

In your opinion, who was more heroic, Astor or

Guggenheim?

Is it true that Bruce Ismay dressed in women's clothes to get on a lifeboat?

She tried to give them the answers they wanted but kept the truth to herself.

It would be impossible to single out one person, when they all died that someone else might live. And I don't know or care what Mr Ismay did to survive. Would you or I have done differently in his shoes?

Shaking her head to banish all thoughts of the *Titanic*, Bertha leaned further out of the window, so she could see Posy chomping on grass in the paddock. Her promised pony was grey, not chestnut, and more sedate than feisty, but Bertha adored her. In fact, she adored everything about her new life. It would be perfect if it wasn't for the flashbacks. Anything could set those off. When Mrs Perkins lit fireworks to welcome her new neighbours, Bertha was suddenly watching flares explode like white stars over the deck of the *Titanic*. When someone whistled Alexander's Ragtime Band, she was crouched on Lifeboat Number 9, watching the horror unfold, listening to the screams of a thousand people drowning.

Her father called again, his voice booming like a foghorn.

'Get yourself down here, lass! You're missing a beautiful day.'

Bertha leapt down from the window seat and pulled

her favourite dress from her closet.

Every day seemed to be beautiful here, and although her father said winter had been wet and chilly, it was hard to imagine that this place could ever be as grey as Aberdeen.

Tugging on her stockings, buttoning her pinafore dress, Bertha tried to focus on getting ready to keep the memories at bay, but they flooded in, unstoppable this morning.

Bertha could hardly bear to picture the haunted expression on Madge's face the last time she'd seen her; on Pier 54 as they'd disembarked from the *Carpathia*. The ship had arrived in New York Harbour, accompanied by flashes of lightning, crashing thunder, teeming rain and dozens of small boats filled with newspaper reporters, who used megaphones to yell at *Carpathia*'s passengers and crew.

How many on board?

They'd arrived at the White Star Line's Pier and had disembarked almost immediately. Blinding lights had flashed in their faces. A sea of reporters had surged towards them.

How many survivors? How many dead? Is it true the officers were shooting passengers? Is it true that an officer killed himself?

Charlotte Collyer had stumbled as they'd walked down the gangway and Bertha's mother had taken her arm.

'Let's keep our heads high and ignore them,' she'd said. 'They're nothing but vultures.'

But as they'd stepped onto the dock, Charlotte had pulled away.

'They'll pay for my story, Mrs Watt. We're going to need the money.'

And she'd drifted away from them, towards the camera's flashing bulbs, Madge clinging to her coat, both looking hopelessly lost.

When Bertha skidded out of the back door, her father was clipping the hedge, and her mother was sipping tea in the arbour, her basket and secateurs at her feet. She waved Bertha over.

'Oh you're up at last! Come and see this! I'm sure you'll be interested!'

Bertha hovered on the path. She wanted to go and see Posy. And her mother's interesting object was probably another plant. Her mother was always discovering unfamiliar American flowers or shrubs in the garden, and was determined to identify them, but Bertha didn't find the whole business of detection nearly as thrilling as she once had, and *The Collyer-Watt Detective Agency's* casebook was at the bottom of the sea. Although it had to be said, *The Mystery of Mr Hoffman and the Case of the Treasure Map* had been much more exciting than *Do you think this flower's a hellebore or a heliotrope?*

But her mother had her reading glasses perched on the end of her nose, and was waving a newspaper.

'Come and read the headline in the New York Times! You'll hardly believe it!'

Bertha leaned over her mother's shoulder so she could see, but it was the picture which drew her eye. Her hands flew to her face.

'It's Lolo and Momon!'

She peered at the photograph.

'Is that their mother?'

She knew it was, of course she did. The woman cuddling the boys had big, dark eyes and curly hair. Her smile was one of pure joy.

The newspaper article explained it all, and as Bertha read it aloud, she discovered that her detective skills had not let her down.

'There *was* something fishy going on! I knew it!'

She read on, shaking her head in amazement.

Louis Hoffman had been an assumed name. The man they'd buried in the Jewish Cemetery in Halifax wasn't Jewish at all. Mr Hoffman's real name had been Michel Navratil Senior and he was a Hungarian tailor who had moved to France when he married his wife, Marcelle. And Marcelle wasn't dead. She was very much alive.

'I could tell right away that there was something

peculiar about Mr Hoffman! I knew he was hiding a dark secret!'

For the first time since the tragedy, Bertha didn't try to shut the past in a box. It felt extremely satisfying that the detectives of *The Collyer-Watt Agency* had been proved right. Somehow, she must let Madge know. She'd meant to write to her, enclosing a copy of the letter she'd sent to Francis and Emily, when she'd posted Alice's photo. But now she could send the newspaper cutting and tell Madge that both the agency's cases had been satisfactorily resolved. It was lovely to imagine Madge bouncing on the spot as she read Bertha's letter, excitement dancing in her eyes.

That's so wonderful, Bertha! I knew we'd have a happy ending!

'Keep reading,' urged Bertha's mother. 'The article continues on page 5.'

As Bertha read on, the pages lifted, rustling in the breeze. She held the paper down on the table with both hands, and squinted as she read the tiny print.

Navratil and his wife were going through a divorce. At the Easter weekend, the boys, whose real names were Michel and Edmond, went to stay with their father, but when Marcelle came to get them, they'd disappeared. Navratil had snatched his sons, taken them by boat and train to Southampton and boarded the *Titanic*, planning to start a new life with the boys in America. Their mother had been utterly distraught but had no idea what had happened to her sons, and was convinced she'd never see them again.

Bertha looked up from the newspaper, her eyes shining.

'Imagine Madame Navratil's amazement when she saw the boys' photograph in the newspapers,' she said, clapping her hands in delight at the thought. 'Imagine her joy when she realised they were safe!'

Bertha's mother smiled.

'It's lovely to see the sparkle back in your eyes, dear. And you're right to be glad. Amid all the horror and the tragedy, those little boys have the happiest ending possible. And don't forget you helped to bring about this reunion. It was you who reunited the two boys on the *Carpathia*.'

Bertha chewed on her lip. She hadn't mentioned Johan, she just said she'd spotted Momon wandering around on the steerage deck and had gone down and rescued him. At the time, it had seemed sensible, and her explanation had been readily accepted, but now it felt unfair, as if she was grabbing the glory for herself.

She placed the newspaper down on the garden table, and walked towards the paddock where Posy was chomping grass. As soon as she approached, the pony trotted over and stuck her head over the bars of the gate, nudging Bertha's arm, hoping for a carrot.

Bertha buried her head in the pony's silky mane, breathing in her warmth, letting the torrent of memories slow to a steady trickle: Lolo and Momon playing chase with her and Madge; standing on the *Titanic*'s deck in their matching coats; Lolo's lost, haunted expression when he was left alone on the *Carpathia*. And she remembered the proud smile on Johan's face when he'd stood on the deck, holding Momon's hand.

He knew he'd found the treasure, and in the end, that was all that mattered.

~The End~

Afterword

Robertha Josephine Watt (Bertha)

In September 1912, Bertha started classes at Jefferson High School. Later she attended Oregon Agricultural College. While Bertha was at high school she wrote a detailed account of her experiences on the Titanic for the school newspaper. After college, she became a bookkeeper.

In 1923, she married Leslie Frederick Marshall, a Canadian dentist. After her marriage, Bertha moved to Vancouver and became a Canadian citizen. She had three sons, who all became dentists, and one daughter, Jane. Bertha and her husband owned a yacht, and often went on sailing holidays.

In 1963, she wrote a long letter to Walter Lord about the Titanic, criticizing inaccuracies in his book, *A Night to Remember*. Bertha died in Vancouver aged 93, the last remaining Scottish Canadian survivor of the Titanic.

Marjorie Collyer (Madge)

Madge travelled to Idaho with her mother Charlotte, but Charlotte remained in poor health and struggled to start up the fruit farm alone. They returned to England, where Charlotte remarried in 1914, but sadly died of tuberculosis in 1916, leaving Madge orphaned. Her step father cared for her until his death in 1916, after which Madge was brought up by an uncle, until she married in 1927. Tragically, her husband Roy died, aged only 41. Madge did not remarry and worked as a doctor's receptionist in Surrey. She died in a Hampshire Nursing Home aged 61.

In 1955, Madge wrote '*Since that time (the Titanic's sinking) I have been blessed with bad luck and often wonder if it will ever give me a break, but it just seems to be my lot.*'

Johan Cervin Svensson

When he arrived in America, Johan changed his name to John C. Johnson. For several years he worked as a farmhand for his father at the family farm in Garfield, Clay County, South Dakota. All of his siblings followed him to America, but sadly Johan's mother died in Knäred, Sweden in 1914, and so he never saw her again.

Johan/John married twice. He finally settled in

California, where he worked as a ship's welder, and he and his second wife Hazel had a daughter named Joy. He died in 1981 aged 82.

Mrs Rosa Pinsky

Rosa needed hospital care after her ordeal on the Titanic and, after receiving 200 dollars from the Red Cross, returned to Europe to stay with relatives.

Miss Ellen Toomey

On her arrival in America, Ellen went to live in Indianapolis with her sisters, but soon moved into a convent where she stayed for the rest of her life.

Nils Martin Odahl

Nils died, aged 23, in the sinking and his body, if recovered, was never identified.

Reginald Ivan Pacey

Reginald (2nd Class lift attendant on the Titanic),

died, aged 17, in the sinking and his body, if recovered, was never identified.

Louis Hoffman

Louis Hoffman (real name Michel Navratil Snr) died in the sinking. He was presumed to be Jewish, so was buried in the Baron de Hirsch Cemetry in Halifax.

His sons Michel and Edmond Navratil (Lolo and Momon) returned to France with their mother aboard the *Titanic*'s sister ship, the *Oceanic*.

Edmond suffered poor health after his experiences as a prisoner-of-war in the Second World War and died in the early 1950s aged 43. Michel became a professor of philosophy and lived to the age of 92, one of the last survivors of the sinking of the *Titanic*.

In total, 1496 passengers and crew died in the sinking and there were 712 survivors.
(figures from encyclopedia-titanic.org)

Of the 107 children on board the Titanic, 50 died.

Marjorie Collyer (Madge) with her mother
Charlototte Collyer after the sinking

Mrs. Charlotte Collyer, 1912 Source: Library of Congress Author: Bain News Service, publisher Permission: No known restrictions on publication. This image is available from the United States Library of Congress's Prints and Photographs division under the digital ID ggbain.19397.

Robertha Josephine Watt (Bertha)

(Public domain)

Last Lifeboat (Opposite)

Last lifeboat arrived, filled with Titanic survivors. This photograph was taken by a passenger of the Carpathia, the ship that received the Titanic's distress signal and came to rescue the survivors. It shows the last lifeboat successfully launched from the Titanic. (Public domain)

Michel Marcel Navratil, and his younger brother, Edmond Roger.

Taken in April 1912 to publish in newspapers in order to assist in their identification. (Public domain)

Acknowledgements

With grateful thanks to:

Anne Glennie at Cranachan Publishing, for being so enthusiastic about this book from the start, and for designing such a fabulous cover.

Kelly MacDonald, and all of the #Clan Cranachan authors. It's lovely to be part of such a proactive and supportive group. Looking forward to reading all of the new books coming out this year!

The Titanic Museum in Belfast, for being a brilliant source of inspiration and information.

Julie Paterson, Literacy Development Officer at Renfrewshire Council and Andrew Givan, Co-ordinator for Children's Library Services in Renfrewshire, for being so supportive.

Fiona Pollok, for reading the first draft and being so kind about it.

My amazing colleagues at Kilbarchan Primary, who are a wonderful team and should never forget it.

All my lovely wee pupils, past and present, who have made teaching an absolute pleasure. Keep reading!

My darling mum and dad, sisters Lesley, Susan and Alison and brother Andrew, my partner Ian and Sally, Keith, David, Ruth, Matt and Emily. Love you all to bits. xx

You might also enjoy

The Beast on the Broch
by John K. Fulton
Scotland, 799 AD. Talorca befriends a strange Pictish
beast; together, they fight off Viking raiders.

Charlie's Promise
by Annemarie Allan
A frightened refugee arrives in Scotland on the
brink of WW2 and needs Charlie's help.

Fir for Luck
by Barbara Henderson
The heart-wrenching tale of a girl's courage to save her
village from the Highland Clearances.

A Pattern of Secrets
by Lindsay Littleson
Jim must save his brother from the Poor House in
this gripping Victorian mystery.

Punch
by Barbara Henderson
Runaway Phin's journey across Victorian Scotland with
an escaped prisoner and a dancing bear.

The Revenge of Tirpitz
by M. L. Sloan
The thrilling WW2 story of a boy's role in the sinking
of the warship Tirpitz.